A CHRISTMAS SPARK

CINDY STEEL

*For Lisa—who shares my love of flirty, sarcastic, and on occasion,
delightfully inappropriate male characters. This book is for you.*

PROLOGUE

I was going to throw up.

The Eugene, Idaho middle school loomed ahead of me on the sidewalk, feeling especially large. My brother, Matt, who had been walking by my side, began to open the door for me and, just as I neared the threshold, shut it in my face. I glanced over at him, annoyed.

"Don't be a butt head."

He laughed, his eyes crinkling as he opened the door once more, this time letting me enter. "What's your deal today? You look like you're going to puke."

I could only agree with him, and the odor assailing us upon entering the side door, in-between the practice gym and cafeteria, was not helping. Judging by the smell of body odor, leather, cheap cologne, and some sort of scrambled egg mixture that wafted in the air, the basketball team must have had their early morning practice and the cafeteria must be serving breakfast. Although these smells didn't help, it wasn't exactly what was causing me to want to upchuck the pop tart I had pecked at for breakfast.

We stopped at a water fountain. Matt leaned down for a drink, while my eyes went unwillingly to the poster hanging above, advertising the Sadie Hawkins Dance in one week. I swallowed hard.

I spotted my best friend, Gina, at the end of the hall, talking to a group of our friends, and suddenly remembered the promise I had made to her. I turned to Matt. "Be sure you check your locker before you go home today."

He didn't stop walking, but he eyed me suspiciously. "Why?"

Despite the pit in my stomach, I comically avoided his gaze. "No reason. Just wanting to be sure you have everything you need before you go home..." I trailed off at the growing wariness in his eyes, because now he understood perfectly what I was telling him.

"She gonna ask me?"

"I don't know what you're talking about."

He sidled up closer to me, flung his arm around my shoulders, and propelled me forward. "Liar."

I contemplated shrugging him off, but truth be told, I had a big day coming up, and any extra support I found in my brother could only help. Sometimes I was amazed we were even twins. We did share our dad's brown eyes and my mom's pert nose, but our similarities stopped there. Matt had a lean, athletic build, dark hair, and an easy smile. I also had a lean build, but there was nothing athletic about my body—no shape and no definition. I just had limbs that frequently fell down, got in the way, and nearly poked eyes out. Matt even had the better hair, which was totally unfair. His was dark, rich, and full, while mine was long and mousy brown, with zero body. I guess that just goes along with my general physical theme—mousy, with no body.

"Who are you asking?"

"Hmm?" I looked over at Matt.

"Are you asking anybody? I can't imagine Gina not forcing you to ask somebody if she is."

"Nobody." No way. Until I got a 'yes' reply, I would take this information to the grave.

"Penny, tell me."

"Maybe nobody. I'll see you later." I pushed him toward some of our friends that were huddled against a locker. Usually, I stayed to chat, but today, I needed to get to Gina. Matt shrugged and turned toward our friends. All of our "friends" already had dates to the dance, so now, I was forced to ask Chase. Okay, maybe 'forced' was pushing it, but he was the only other guy who had given me the time of day. Mind you, it was a very *slight* time of day.

Chase Riley.

Tall, dark hair...he did that thing where, when he smiled, it was a crooked, half-smile out of the side of his mouth. It was like he always had some joke on the tip of his tongue. It might not be everybody's cup of tea, but...

It. Was. Mine.

Once, he dropped his pencil behind his desk in class. When I reached down and handed it back to him, he gave me that crooked smile in thanks, and just like that, social studies became my favorite class. Once, our teacher Mr. Thomas walked in front of the fan, and it blew his hair partially askance on his head.

Did any of us know it was a toupee? Nope.

We had been taking a test that day. Most of the class had been poring over their tests on their desks and hadn't noticed, but Chase and I had been looking up at the same time, and we both saw it. He snickered softly at first, and then I joined in. A while later, while I was writing the essay section for the test, a small piece of paper landed on my desk. I glanced around to make sure Mr. Thomas wasn't looking, before taking in the crudely sketched drawing of our teacher with his hair flying off his head. I snickered.

If I were being honest, I liked our teacher and felt bad for making fun of him. However, Chase Riley had drawn me a note and passed it to me in class.

Me.

I stared at the note, trying to figure out my next move. I changed the face of my teacher on the paper to one of horror and passed it back to him. His shoulders shook with mirth before we went back to our tests. That had been it. He still talked mostly to his friends during class, but every once in a while, he would send me a look when something was funny. So far, I had made him laugh exactly two times.

So...we were friends, right? Friends could ask friends to the dance. The pit in my stomach grew into a tree.

"Penny!"

By that time, I had made my way to where Gina stood next to our shared locker. Her expressive eyes looked me over as I approached. "You feeling okay?"

"I've been better. *Your* fault."

She smiled as she tossed her auburn, Disney princess hair over her shoulder. "You'll be fine. It's not like it's a real date or anything." She wasn't wrong. We were only in the 8th grade. The dance would be held after school because nobody could drive yet. Getting a "date" probably just guaranteed us some dances.

"Did you tell him?" My best friend was busy looking over my shoulder down the hallway, no doubt searching for my twin.

"I didn't tell him. I just told him to check his locker before going home."

"Do you think he'll say yes?"

"Positive. Now can we stop talking about you liking my brother? I already feel like I might puke."

She laughed and opened her locker, rummaging through her bag of toiletries. "Just think, if he says yes, you get to talk to him!"

I leaned against the locker next door. "The keyword here is *'if.'*"

Gina applied a thin coat of lip-gloss, checking herself out in the mirror that was pressed against the inside door. "Did you bring the candy gram?"

"That thing burning a humongous hole in my backpack? Yeah, I brought it." I hadn't wanted to do any sort of grand gesture to ask him to the dance, but Gina insisted we had to do something, so we settled on a candy gram. Everyone liked candy, right? She made one for Matt, and I made one for Chase, which meant we spent all night surrounded by a pile of candy bars, coming up with lines like, 'I love snickering with you in class,' and 'It would be worth 100 Grand if you'd go with me to the dance.'

What have I done?

Gina was not deterred. Of course, it was easier for her; she knew Matt would say yes. Given the general amount of time I have spent actually talking to Chase, his niceness was still up for debate. I nudged Gina to the side and checked my own reflection in the mirror. No new pimples had appeared on my red, blotched cheeks since that morning, and I had no hidden boogers in my nose. I checked for food in my braces and picked out a speck of pop tart.

"The bell's going to ring any minute," Gina said. "Then you go to his locker and I'll go to Matt's, and we'll make the drop."

"Josh said he'd hang around his locker for a minute after the bell, so he can get you in," I told her, clutching the shoulder straps on my backpack as if they were a lifeline. "Did you ask Mike to do the same for me?" Mike was Chase's locker partner.

"He'll be there. He said he might be late, but he'll be there."

The bell rang and we parted ways, each of us carrying our loaded backpacks to our intended lockers. Chase's locker was down in the corner of two connecting hallways surrounding the practice gym. I peered down the hall and saw him, Pete Davis, and Jason Malcolm standing next to his locker, laughing loudly at something. Pete and Jason were both in social studies with us and, while Jason was okay, Pete wasn't my favorite person. I moved to wait in the hallway, located behind his locker until they left. As the middle schoolers began to disperse toward their various classes, their voices became louder. I leaned against the wall running perpendicular behind them, ready to wait it out, just out of sight.

But not out of hearing.

"Jason, I heard Brandi Templeman was gonna ask you to the dance." Pete's laughter took on a higher pitch as if he were doubled over, laughing at the thought. "But she couldn't find a dress big enough to fit her."

The two boys laughed, albeit a bit stiffly.

"Shut up, Davis." That was Chase's voice. Relief warmed my heart. Good, I was glad he was going to put Pete in his place for his mean comment. I had sat next to Brandi in algebra the year previous and we had bonded over our hatred for Mr. Young's surprise pop quizzes he tortured his class with.

"I heard Kat Hunter wanted *your* number," Chase said, laughing.

The boys guffawed while I rolled my eyes, disappointment flooding through me. It felt a bit like watching an interview of a celebrity who played a role in my favorite movie. They were usually a letdown after falling in love with the character they played on screen.

"You better watch out, Riley," Pete added, through the laughter. "I hear that Penny chick from social studies is into you."

I stiffened at the sound of my name. My heart dropped. How could he have heard that? I hadn't told anyone, except Gina, and she would never say anything.

"Penny who?"

Despite being on edge while listening to this conversation, I felt a bit hurt. How could he not know who I was? He had passed me a note! I made him laugh. Twice! Did that mean nothing?

"You know, no boobs. No butt. Boring. Sits behind you."

I covered my hands over my mouth, but no sound came out. I couldn't move. I think I even stopped breathing. My stomach clenched tight and my ears perked up, waiting for more, while at the same time wanting to make a break for it.

"Oh yeah. Now I remember. She looks like my dog, but not as hot."

The boys snorted in laughter. The tardy bell rang, and from a distance, I heard a locker door slam, and the voices faded away as they shuffled toward class. Our class.

My face fell, deflated, along with my heart. I wrapped my hands around my stomach, sliding down the wall to sit with my knees bent. I sat in stunned silence for several minutes, my heart pounding, running the words he had said over and over again in my head; cementing them as a permanent fixture in my brain.

'She looks like my dog, but not as hot.'

What did that even mean? The boys had laughed like they had known what it meant. Those boys who I had sat by, passed papers to, and even smiled at when they made jokes in class. They laughed at me.

Chase had said I looked like a dog. Uglier than a dog. Tears leaked from the corner of my eyes, the sting burning the creases as footsteps sounded down the hallway. I averted my face and discreetly wiped at the tears.

"Penny, are you sick?"

Turning, I looked at Mrs. Norris, the school counselor, as she approached. I nodded up at her, in my dazed stupor. She had a history of wearing the brightest colors imaginable, and today's orange was no different. Her arm jangled with bracelets as she placed her hand on my elbow and helped me to stand.

"Let's go to the office and we'll call your mom."

A few minutes later, I sat alone in the nurse's office, waiting for my mom to pick me up. As if the fates were all conspiring against me, across from where I sat was a full-length mirror. I squinted at myself to get a better view. My brown hair lay limp and stringy just past my shoulders. My braces pushed against my lips, making them poke out just a bit. At my count that morning, I had a total of eleven zits running across my face.

Was it all true?

I had never thought of myself as ugly. I always figured, if I were ugly, my family would have told me. Or at least given me that impression. Even though I compared myself to Matt's good looks, I always figured I would catch up someday. Ugly. What did that word even mean? Why did it hurt so bad that *Chase* had implied it? Was it because I had been so delusional in thinking that he liked me? Not in a girlfriend way, but in a 'friend' kind of way. He had tossed me a secret note. Wasn't that a 'friend' thing to do? Yes, I was about to ask him to a dance, but that was it. I didn't expect anything else. I thought he was cute, but I knew he was out of my league. It all just felt like a giant stab in my bulging backpack full of candy bars and cheesy rhymes. Gina and Matt would be going to the dance without me.

I didn't have boobs. That part was true, though I still remained hopeful. I had no curves. Pete thought I was boring.

Chase thought his dog was hotter than me.

It took several weeks for my fragile, middle school heart to patch itself back together. I had been burned. Tossed into the inferno, only to spit me back out into social studies with Chase and Pete. I no longer held interactions with them beyond the necessities. I didn't laugh at their jokes, I no longer found them funny. Those moments were gone. But there was also a moment—albeit several days later—that begged for the 'Pretty Woman moment.' Gina's mom had that movie in her secret stash that she didn't know we knew about. One afternoon, to cheer me up, Gina snuck it away and we watched it together. There was a moment in that movie when Julia Roberts went back into the high-end store that she was kicked out of days earlier, only to rub it in their faces that she could have bought them out. She showed them that they shouldn't have judged her based on her looks. Then, she had her grand finale statement to the snobby shop workers, where she said, 'Big mistake. Huge.'

Gina and I had cheered when she said that. We had clapped as she spun around and walked away. Maybe that would be me and Chase someday—when I found my confidence. My moment.

First, I had to find out—what could a person be, if not pretty?

1

All four tires on my trusty Toyota Corolla spun loudly, putting up a decent fight. Eventually, they lost the battle. Amidst prayers and swears on my part, I stomped on my brakes to keep from rolling backward and careening off the mountainside. The car slid back a few inches before stopping. I held my breath, muscles tensed, as I tried to figure out my next move. The snow pelted down like a scene from Star Wars. It was also pitch-black outside. Did I mention that? Instead of leaving for the cabin at a sensible time, like three in the afternoon, I left after work. At seven at night. In the winter. During a huge snowstorm.

'Okay, don't panic,' I told myself. 'Stay calm, think.'

My first inclination was to call my dad. Ten years after graduating high school and moving out of my childhood home, I *still* called him to fix all the broken things. I had dated *plenty* of other men (three other men) and nobody responded as promptly, and with such attention to detail, as my dad. He was a 'Jack of all Trades' too. It didn't matter what it was–the garbage disposal, the leaky sink, or the front door that refused to shut properly. Dad could fix it all. Too bad my parents were in London visiting my sister and her husband for the

Christmas holiday. There was nothing he could do from that far away, except worry.

My next thought was to call Gina. After all, she had been the one who invited me to her cabin the week before Christmas. Then I remembered, she was on a cruise with my twin brother Matt and their young family. That's right, my twin brother married my best friend Gina, and we all graduated high school together. We were just one big, happy, All-American family. Well, except, *they* had a family. I did not.

I'm getting off track.

Knowing I would be alone, Gina offered me the use of her family's remote cabin in the mountains of the Salmon-Challis National Forest in Idaho. Once they were back on land, they planned to meet me at the cabin on Christmas Day, to spend the holiday together. I was under a deadline for my third book, and a week by myself in a snowy, cozy, fire drawn cabin had seemed like a slice of heaven.

However, *now*, in the black of night, alone, on a steep, snowy mountain road, all I could think about was serial killers, chainsaws, and...Bigfoot.

The car slid backward a few more inches and I gripped the wheel in alarm.

The only sensible thing for me to do was to park the car somewhere to the right of the road. I could move it the next morning. The cabin couldn't be too much further. If I remembered correctly, the road ended at the cabin, so no other cars should be on the road.

I put the car in reverse and slowly turned my wheel, letting up on the brake slightly. The car jerked backward. Squealing, I slammed on the brakes. To my relief, the car was now in a better position and had inched more toward the mountainside, instead of the cliff.

Once I felt like I was far enough off the main road to park, I turned the car off and eased my foot off the brake, waiting for the ax to fall. Nothing fell. The car miraculously stayed still. A sigh burst from my lungs, and the tension that had built up in my shoulders slowly dissipated.

According to the weather on my car dashboard, it was exactly nine degrees outside. I couldn't see the cabin from where I sat but thought it to be at least a quarter of a mile uphill. The snow looked to be at least twelve inches deep and coming down fast. In the back seat sat my large suitcase, makeup kit, laptop, a box of food, a cooler, and my favorite quilt.

It felt like what I imagined picking my favorite child would be like, as I debated over my necessities for the night. Not that I had any children, but still—if I did—some of them would have to sleep in the car. Okay, I'm kidding, but there was no way I could haul my entire luggage up the hill in the storm.

I finally settled on my toiletry bag, laptop, and my favorite blanket. I needed my laptop to write, my toiletry bag had my bathroom necessities, and my blanket—well, I wasn't sure what the blanket situation was at this cabin, but I wasn't about to be disappointed. I would brave the elements again tomorrow to grab my food. I was just hoping the cabin had a few straggler packs of hot chocolate tucked away somewhere. I cinched up my heavy winter coat and pulled on my snow boots.

Before I grabbed the door handle, I glanced sideways back at my luggage. Buried down deep was a new pair of flannel pajamas I bought while envisioning cozy nights writing by the fire. I wasn't in the mood to try to open the case in the tiny backseat of my car, on a dark mountainside, to rifle through for them. The warm, fuzzy pajamas would have to wait.

The cold bit at my lungs as I stepped out of the car. The chill settled quickly and deeply into my bones. I wrapped my blanket around my head and body, attempting to shield the onslaught of snow pelting my face. I locked my car and soon after, the interior lights turned off, leaving me all alone in utter darkness. I suddenly felt very small and appetizing in the vast and terrifying world before me.

Snack-size.

My hands fumbled with the flashlight on my phone. When the singular light lit a tunnel through the suffocating black, I wasted no time moving. The snow crunched beneath my feet, no doubt alerting some fearsome creature to my whereabouts. Under the security of my quilt, I braved the elements to peer out into the night. The darkened trees stood, glaring ominously at me, as I trudged my way forward.

What a lovely time to suddenly remember *every* detail of *every* scary movie I had ever watched. A strange noise sounded in the distance. Was that just my imagination? No... There it was again. That sounded an awful lot like...

That was *not* a chainsaw.

I quickened my pace, which only made me feel ridiculous as I waddled faster, burdened under the weight of my necessities for the night. A large and forbidding tree loomed ahead of me—curved in just a way that made my breath hitch.

Keep walking. It's just a tree. Bigfoot isn't real. Just because I saw a TV show about him when I was a kid doesn't mean it's real.

Just because there have been thousands of reported sightings doesn't mean...

A howl sounded in the distance.

A wolf.

A *wolf* was howling.

I dropped all pretense of calm and bolted forward, my bags and blanket trying to slow me down, but failing; adrenaline could be a wonderful thing. Rounding the bend in the road, a small, darkened cabin emerged before me. I had been there once before with Gina, but it had been years. Even in the unnerving, forest night, the cabin stood out like something in a fairy tale. It was simple in its coziness. It wasn't tall or large, but it had the essence of an Old Mother Hubbard's touch. A porch wrapped around the front of the cabin, with a chimney atop the roof. The small stream of smoke drifting out into the night seemed a welcome sight.

Another howl from the wolf had me scrambling to the door. I jammed the key in the lock to no avail. I tried the second key-nothing. On my fourth attempt, I cursed Gina and Matt and all their children. Finally, the fifth time proved charming, and the door creaked open.

A strong smell of bacon assailed me when I stepped inside and closed the door. I fumbled around for the light switch and found it hidden behind a heavy Carhartt coat and some straggler jackets, hanging on hooks by the door. A dim, yellow light cut through the darkness, casting a cozy glow about the living room. A hand-me-down plaid couch sat just in front of the door, facing an old TV that sat on a stand against the wall. A blue recliner with a deep indent in the seat sat perpendicular to the couch. Just past the living room was a small kitchen nook, with a table big enough for four, pushed against the right side of the wall.

A blanket lay haphazardly across the couch, beckoning me closer. The tension-filled night had drained me, and all I found myself wanting was to brush my teeth and devour a cup of hot chocolate. Although, not in that order. My flannel pajamas would have been the third thing, but I would not be stepping outside again until the sun was up, and even that was negotiable. I flung my bags and coat onto the couch and walked into the kitchen.

A pan, with a pool of bacon grease, sat on the stove along with a dirty plate and fork in the sink. I furrowed my brows slightly but was too tired to care about a neglectful cleaning service. I rummaged through a few cupboards until I found a mug and filled it with water, sipping gratefully. The glass clunked against the counter as I set it down and turned in pursuit of the master bedroom, nearly tripping over a duffle bag sitting next to the back of the couch.

Looking back, I assume that a more sound-minded person would have picked up on all of the—smack to the head— clues that I wasn't alone in that cabin. The smoke in the chimney, the bacon, the plates, the bag... I just thought the cleaners hadn't been able to get to the cabin; I had barely made it through the storm myself. I had just been through the harrowing ordeal of nearly plunging off the mountain-side in the middle of the night, and I was trying not to think about wild animals and chainsaw murderers. I think my brain skipped over a few details to keep me feeling safe. It was survival.

Or perhaps that's what all the victims say.

Or would have said.

To the right, between the kitchen and the living room, was a small hallway with four doors. From my time spent there years ago, I knew that one door led to the small laundry room, and the other three housed a bathroom and two bedrooms. I rounded the bend, turning down the hallway to pick my room when the bathroom door was yanked open. Smoke and steam infiltrated the small passageway, before a completely naked man, except a small towel wrapped around his hips, stepped out into the hallway.

For a brief second, I stood, stunned at how the sudden appearance of finely chiseled abs and arm muscles had made their way into my snowy mountain escape. I mean, in that brief second, I saw that sexy 'V' thing on his abdomen. But, once the image of the gloriously half-naked man reached the functioning part of my brain, my illusion of safety shattered.

We saw each other at the same time—each of us yelping and jumping backward in surprise. The man smacked into the door frame of the bathroom, while I slammed against the wall.

The naked man was the first to get ahold of his senses. "Holy crap! Who are you!?"

"Me? Who are you?" I jumped up and flew down the hallway, rounding to the other side of the couch, putting distance between me and his nakedness.

Don't look back, I told myself. *Do not look at his abs. Don't. Get ready to run. You can take your chances with the wolves.* My hand felt the small bulge of keys in my right pocket.

"Wait. Do I know you?"

My head jerked up as I grabbed for my laptop, pausing my plan for a hasty retreat. The man tilted his head to the side, taking me in with a puzzled look on his face. At a second glance, it was a very familiar face.

"Blister?"

2

Instantly, I no longer felt physically afraid; but in that one word, I was fourteen again—in all of its pimply, gangly, braces-clad, frizzy-haired glory. I wasn't sure which was worse.

No way.

No *way*.

Only one imbecile on this earth would call me 'Blister,' and I refused to accept that the pair of incredulous eyes staring at me belonged to him. Then it opened its mouth again.

"Blister! What are you doing here? You scared the crap out of me." Good gracious, why was he looking at me as though he'd been given bacon and eggs for breakfast when he'd ordered oatmeal?

"It's Penny."

"What?"

"My name. It's Penny." I spoke slowly, so as not to confuse him.

"Right," he said, his eyes roaming over me. "Sorry. Old habits. I haven't seen you since... When was it? Matt and Gina's wedding?"

Of all the things I was not in the mood for at that moment, rehashing the last time I saw Chase Riley was at the very top of my list. No matter that he looked like some sort of Greek God standing before me without his shirt on. Eyes up, Penny.

"What are you doing here, Chase?" I folded my arms, trying to look more in control of this situation than I felt.

His eyebrows rose as he leaned against the wall. "Me? I was taking a shower. In *my* cabin."

"No, no. *My* cabin. Gina gave me permission to use it this week."

He shrugged. "Matt gave me the keys."

"No."

He held up his hands and spoke slowly as if trying to calm down a psychotic animal. "I paid Matt two weeks ago when he gave me the keys for this week."

"I talked to Gina..." My voice trailed off as my mind exploded. No. No. No.

I strode to the window and peered through the blinds to see the winter snow warning up close and personal. I imagined myself grabbing my bags, tossing Chase a wave, and stalking out toward my car in a very confident huff. I considered the pros and cons between a Bigfoot encounter or staying in the same cabin as Chase. Bigfoot might be hairy and gross enough for the two of us, but at least he would probably never think to call me a dog. Bigfoot would have never known that, after an unfortunate incident in the ninth grade, my nickname in some circles at school became Blister. On the flip side...Chase probably wouldn't eat me. Although to be fair, I'm not really sure what Bigfoot does beyond just making people crap their pants at the sight of him. Does he eat people?

Wait. Why was I worried about *me*? Chase should be the one leaving. This was *my* cabin for the week. Besides, all my fake bravado aside, not even Chase Riley could make me leave at this hour and traipse down the mountain to my car, which was probably buried in snow.

"I'll call her." My fingers itched for something to do to make this all go away. I pulled my phone out of my pocket; Gina would not stand for this. Surely, she would kick Chase out, maybe give him a free stay another week.

"Don't bother. There's no service. And they're on their cruise, so they wouldn't be able to answer. My guess is that neither one told the other."

"You think, genius?" I stared at my phone, begging it to magically make Chase disappear.

"You look different. Your hair is darker."

He had a hint of a smirk on his face as if he were reliving a funny memory. Guaranteed, some memory I had no interest in reliving at the present moment. Presently, I needed those abs out of my face, and him fully dressed.

"Listen, I know we need to figure this out, but could you go put some clothes on?"

He arched a teasing eyebrow. "Driving you wild, huh?"

I refused to show him any weakness. "More like blinding me, whitey."

He grinned and bowed, before disappearing into one of the back rooms. When the door clicked shut, I sunk onto the couch and blew out my first breath of air since the bathroom door opened two minutes before. That was a lie. He didn't have a stitch of white on his whole body that I could tell, and *almost* fully against my will, I had gotten a close look. Too bad he was an idiot.

The fireplace in front of me showed signs of a fire earlier in the day, but it had since gone out, leaving the air inside the cabin chilly. I rubbed my hands over my arms to allow some blood flow.

What was I going to do?

There was no way I could stay in the cabin alone with Chase. I had a month's worth of writing to do this week, and I needed a quiet, cozy cabin, with zero distractions. Given my past history with Chase, I knew it was impossible for him to not be distracting. And annoying.

The bedroom door opened, and Chase stepped out in a pair of loose-fitting sweats and an old Green Day T-Shirt. I tried to not be jealous of those sweatpants. They looked so warm and comfortable. A step below flannels. He rubbed his hand through his wet hair as he sat on the recliner facing the couch. The shock had worn off and left me feeling very unsettled.

"Well, I guess my quiet week of ice fishing has been shot to blazes now, huh?"

"Not necessarily. You are welcome to leave and come back in a week when I'm gone." I smiled sweetly at him.

He scoffed. "I've decided that even though you might be a pervert or an ax murderer—because it's so late—I'll allow you to stay the night. One night. We can send you on your way in the morning, but I will be sleeping with my door locked, so don't get any ideas."

I narrowed my eyes at him. "I have just as much permission as you have to be here. More so, since this cabin belongs to Gina's family, not Matt's."

"How do you figure that?"

"Matt is my brother and your best friend, but Gina's *my* sister-in-law *and* my best friend. Not yours."

"That's harsh."

I continued, fully aware of the growing gleam in his eyes, and my pathetic argument. "This is her family's cabin, therefore, her word is stronger than Matt's."

"We may be able to figure this out right now. I have my receipt for my payment. Matt was so kind to give me one for tax purposes. It's just in my bag. If you could just show me your receipt saying you also paid for your week stay, then we'll know for sure."

Gina had refused to accept payment, and it would seem that the dirty dog standing before me knew this. I raised my chin a fraction higher. "I don't have it on me."

He leaned back in the recliner, folding his arms, really enjoying himself at my expense. "You don't have it because you didn't pay for it, or because you forgot it?"

"I don't have it on me," I repeated, resisting the urge to snarl.

He bit his lip to keep his smile from growing any broader. "That's too bad."

I cleared my throat. "Which room is mine?"

"That depends on whether you're a pervert or an ax murderer." He grinned at me. "I'd definitely prefer one over the other."

"If I were you, I *would* lock your door tonight," I said, as I brushed past him toward the two bedrooms and grabbed my laptop off the couch. The room to the right of the bathroom was empty, so I stormed inside and slammed the door shut behind me.

The room was small, barely big enough to fit a queen-size bed and a small dresser in the corner. There was one window and a full-length mirror that hung on the wall behind the door. I put the laptop bag onto the moose-and-bear-covered bedspread.

Dang it.

I didn't have any clothes with me. I sat down, the bed squeaking as it accepted my full weight. Why did I stalk into the bedroom first? I should have grabbed my makeup bag and gone into the bathroom. Now, I'm going to have to walk back out and face Chase again to get my toiletry bag. I sat there for a few moments, hoping to make it seem like I had been doing important things.

I opened the door and exited the room at the same time Chase was walking out of the bathroom. Our shoulders bumped in the tight quarters.

"Whoops," he mumbled as he turned and looked at me. "I'm done in there."

"Thanks," I said over my shoulder, as I walked into the living room and grabbed my makeup kit off the couch.

As I made my way back toward the bathroom, he stopped just inside of his doorway and motioned toward the bag in my hand. "Light packer, huh? I'll bet you have all your clothes vacuumed packed in nice little Tetris size bundles. It will make it nice and easy for packing to go home tomorrow."

My eyes narrowed at him, "I'm not going home. If you are any sort of gentleman at all, you would."

He smiled and shook his head. "I think we both know that I'm not. Goodnight, Blister." Before I could get another word in, he closed his door.

There is something so intimate about sharing a bathroom with someone. Are they the type to leave all their things lying around? Dirty underwear? Flicks of toothpaste on the mirror? Would they steal my shampoo? Pick up their towels? Leave smudges inside the toilet? Yuck. Or heaven forbid, leave any sort of hairs...anywhere.

Shudder.

At first glance, Chase seemed quite tidy. The mirror was still partially fogged, but it looked clean enough. There was no underwear or dirty towels on the floor. The only clue he left behind of his presence was a small toiletry bag sitting on the counter, which was unzipped. After a quick and very innocent peek inside, I saw a toothbrush, toothpaste, floss, and a razor, haphazardly strewn about it. There was more stuff, but that was as far as I could see from my vantage point. Don't worry, I didn't touch anything. (I'm not a psycho, just curious).

My hands were like ice when I turned on the shower. I had been blessed with my mother's small frame, which never seemed to warm up in the winter. I undressed quickly, double-checking the lock on the bathroom door. Once hot steam filled the room, I stepped inside, sighing gratefully as my body began to thaw. Other than warming me up, this shower would prove nearly pointless on the cleanliness scale, since I had no clean underwear in the cabin.

I stood under the hot spray for a good ten minutes, trying very hard not to think about Chase. Which was nearly impossible when I was staring at his green bar of Irish Spring soap and shampoo.

Gina would be hearing a strongly worded complaint from me when this week was over.

Yes. Week. If anybody was leaving, it would be him. First of all, as pathetic as it sounded, I had nowhere to go except an empty house. Being away at a semi-empty cabin the week before Christmas seemed more exciting than the brutal reminder that I was, in fact, alone during the holidays. At least until Matt and Gina joined me on Christmas. A quiet week in a beautiful location, where I could write, and hopefully meet my deadline, was just what I needed. If Chase couldn't handle it, then he could leave.

I washed and rinsed my hair, loofah'd my body, and braced myself for the cold chill that I would inevitably face once the water was shut off and I had to open the curtain to grab my towel. The worst part of showering. Once dressed, I de-tangled my long hair, darkened even more by the water, peed, brushed my teeth, removed my contacts, and replaced them with my glasses. Chase mentioned noticing that my hair was darker now. Years earlier, I had opted for a darker shade of brown and never looked back. Matt and I now looked more like twins than ever before—and I felt it gave my face a much less mouse-like appearance. I opened the door, checked all the locks in the house, turned off the kitchen light, and breezed past Chase's closed door. His lights were off, and all was quiet as I locked myself into my room.

I would have given my right kidney to be wearing my flannel pajamas to bed. The box of food in my car, brimming with carbs like mac and cheese and bread, taunted me. It was midnight, but I was a snacky night-eater, and a few crackers sounded divine. Oh well, no matter. All of it could be overlooked, except those pajamas.

The day was beginning to catch up to me, so instead of writing for a few minutes as I had planned, I ignored the laptop sitting in the case and peeled off my jeans and shirt. A flimsy, white tank top and my underwear were not the pajamas of choice while trapped in a cabin with a man, but they were the best I could do. I checked the lock on my door once more, turned out the light, and slid under the covers. I prayed to the heavens above that there were no spiders lurking in the wooden walls of this tiny room.

———

The clock on my phone read 2 am. My muscles ached from shaking so hard. Somewhere during the past two hours, my body heat had dissipated and left my tank-top clad body freezing at the drop in temperature. I shined my phone flashlight all around the room, looking for another blanket to add on top of the thin, moose and bear bedspread. My light landed on the dresser in the corner. I psyched myself up for ten seconds before I leaped out of bed like a ninja. After checking every drawer, I wanted to cry. No blanket. I glanced longingly at the crumpled quilt I had brought in from the car, but it was still wet from my snowy trek to the cabin.

The wall had a thermostat, but every attempt I made to turn on some sort of heat failed. I threw on my jeans and gently turned the doorknob. The house stood silent and undisturbed. Chase's door was still shut. The air was no warmer out there than in my bedroom as I crept out into the living room. I shined my light around the cabin, looking for anything that could give me warmth.

The fireplace had long since died, but even my search for wood came up empty. Even if I found wood, I didn't see any matches, and there was no way on this snow-covered earth that I would be knocking on Chase Riley's door, at two in the morning, to ask him for anything.

Plan B involved me wrapping the nasty tablecloth from the kitchen around my body for warmth if I found nothing else better. My eyes scanned the room and landed on a large trunk on the side of the couch. A moment later, I opened the trunk, praying that nothing furry or leggy would jump out at me when a soft, fuzzy blanket filled my view. It had seen a few years, and very likely, a few hundred house guests, but it may as well have been from heaven. I yanked it out of the box, flipped it out a few times (hopefully releasing any spiders nestled in its yarn), and wrapped it around my body before scampering back to my room. In my rush to get away, my blanket flipped and hit the open trunk just hard enough for the lid to slam shut. I yelped at the sound but wasted no time running back to my room and shutting the door as quickly as I could, without slamming it.

I was in the process of re-wrapping the blanket around my body when I heard Chase's door open. My body tensed. I wasn't sure why I felt nervous, but sneaking out in the dark living room and rushing back to my room made me feel as though I had done something wrong.

"Blister?" A whisper sounded outside my door.

I rolled my eyes. I wasn't answering to that.

"Penny?"

"What?"

"Are you okay? I heard a loud noise."

Ugh. Light sleeper. "Yeah, I'm fine. It was me. Sorry."

There was a long pause before he added, "Is there a dead body in there?"

"I can't tell you unless you want to be next."

There was a dramatic sigh before he said, "You know, I really hoped you weren't a murderer."

I smiled in spite of myself. "Goodnight, moron."

"Night, Blister."

For some reason, the world's tightest and most uncomfortable jeans did not lend themselves to a good night's sleep. They did provide extra warmth, even though that contribution did very little. Even the extra blanket wrapped around me failed to ward off the chill that was so saturated into my body. The wind had picked up sometime in the night, causing my window to rattle, keeping my already tender nerves on high alert. Finally, somewhere between the hours of four and five, the full-body shakes subsided, and I slept.

3

I awoke to the smell of bacon.

Glorious, mouthwatering, flesh of a pig—bacon.

Even though I could, in fact, resist the bacon if I had to, and I felt much safer locked inside my freezing room, unfortunately, I had to pee. I refused to be any sort of die-hard, if it meant me squat-hovering over the tiny trash can in my room. My phone said it was nearly 9 am and my stomach groaned in agony. Before my mind could question my motives, my bladder had me beelining toward the bathroom. I used the facilities, washed my hands, splashed water on my face, and refused to add makeup—because I didn't care what Chase thought—and reached for the door to open it. Instead, I turned back to the mirror to apply a quick coat of mascara, (it's hardly anything and it made ME feel better, but I still didn't care about him at all) and then I exited the bathroom.

I found him in the kitchen, wearing jeans and a flannel button-down shirt, scooping a pile of bacon and a couple of fried eggs onto a plate. He turned, his eyes taking me in, before handing me the plate.

"Morning, Blister. I thought you could use some breakfast before you hit the road."

"Thank you." I smiled sweetly and took the plate, sitting down at the table. "But I'm not leaving." I had spent most of my frozen night stewing over the thought. I didn't want to be here with Chase, but I had nothing to get home to. I had a deadline to meet and... nothing to get home to.

He stole a piece of bacon off my plate as he sat down across from me at the table. "I figured you'd say that. How's this going to work then?"

I swallowed my mouthful of eggs. "How about we just pretend like the other isn't here? We don't even have to talk to each other. Let's just go about our own business and let go of any sort of pressured socialization for what this is. I have a big deadline due in a couple of weeks, and I was counting on being here to get most of it finished. I promise I'll be quiet, but I need to be here."

His eyes laughed at me. "You really think you'll be able to resist talking to me?"

I leaned forward, my hand clutching a piece of bacon. "I managed it *wonderfully* well the past ten years."

He leaned back in his chair and crossed his legs. "I don't know, it just seems awfully convenient that you just *accidentally* show up at the cabin after all this time...right as I'm taking a shower..." He trailed off with a knowing look.

I refused to take his bait. "No. That's not... I didn't..." When he began to laugh, I added, "I'll bet you knew I was coming and planned the whole shower thing. Just to get me..." I stopped, realizing I was coming very close to trapping myself in his snares.

"Just to get you *what*?" His eyes lit up and a tantalizing smile broke across his face.

"Stop it." I leaned forward and slapped him on the side of his face with my bacon. He ducked away, laughing. My face began to feel heated, but I jumped up and walked to the sink to get a glass of water because I was very...thirsty.

When I sat back down again, his brown eyes met mine. "You became a writer, then?"

"Yes."

"For what? Books?"

"Yes."

He seemed mildly impressed. "Really? How many books have you written?"

"I'm writing my third one now."

"What are they about?"

Nope. No way. I gave him a crisp smile. "I don't think we're tight enough for that information."

He cocked his eyebrows. "I'm suddenly very intrigued."

I felt my face turn pink as I turned away and bit a piece of bacon. For all he wasn't, the man could cook bacon perfectly crisp, but that didn't mean I was going to discuss my romance novels with him.

"Where have you been since high school?" I asked him instead. I'd be lying if I said I hadn't kept a few tabs on Chase Riley since graduation. He was best friends with my brother, after all. But, the less he thought I knew, the better.

"Marines," he said, smiling at me.

"Doing what?" I stood and moved back to the sink, shoveling the last bite of eggs into my mouth. I had to move away from his beautiful smile as his intense eyes focused on me.

There was a silence before my skin broke into goosebumps when his voice tickled my ear. "I don't think we're tight enough for that information," he whispered.

Startled, I shoved my elbow back, landing right into his stomach. I only heard his breath catch, but it was enough for me. I whirled around to face him. "If we are going to co-exist in this cabin, rule number one is: don't sneak up on me."

He took a step back, his hands in his pocket and his eyes full of mischief.

I gave him a withering stare. "Don't even think about it. Hey, is the heater in your room working?"

"Yeah, why?"

"I froze last night, mine wouldn't turn on."

His eyes widened before he turned and strode toward my bedroom. I breathed a small sigh of relief with him out of the room. It had been a long time since I had been around Chase, but he took up the entire room with his personality. I plucked the last piece of bacon off the pan on the stove and took a bite.

"It's the breaker," he called from the hallway.

I turned to face him, leaning against the counter. "The breaker?"

He appeared around the corner, a slight chagrined look on his face. "I had to turn my heat on when I got here, and since I wasn't planning on using the second room, I kept it off. I didn't even think about that last night. I just turned it on now."

Cue another palm to the face. That was something I could have fixed myself. "I wish I would have thought of that last night, while I was freezing to death."

He walked back to the kitchen and took a seat on the top of the table. He leaned back, his hands resting on the table behind him. "If you were cold, you could have come snuggled with me."

I took in his alluring, self-assured smile with disgust. "Let me be clear. I wouldn't snuggle with you if you had just donated a kidney to save my grandpa's life. Okay?"

I didn't think it was possible, but his smile grew even wider at my words. Everything was such a game to him.

"I've missed your sweet talk. When does our no talking rule start?"

"Right after I finish eating your bacon." I smiled sweetly and took another bite of the pig flesh in my hand.

He looked up toward the ceiling, blowing out a breath that sounded suspiciously like a laugh. "So many inappropriate thoughts running through my head. Probably best you stop talking. One question though— what are you planning on eating all week?"

Noticing my widened eyes, he continued, "I mean, I always enjoy making a lady breakfast in the morning, but that was the least amount of action I've ever gotten at a sleepover."

"I highly doubt that."

He grinned and raised his eyebrows.

"You're such a pig."

"Did you pack food? Because other than some packs of hot chocolate and a few questionable cans of oatmeal, this cabin is seriously lacking in stuff to eat. Matt told me I had to pack all my food in, but I wasn't planning on feeding an extra person."

I bristled a bit at that comment. I had just as much right as he had to be here. "I was just heading out to get it."

He looked incredulous as he glanced toward the window. "Where?"

"My car is parked down the road a bit. It couldn't make it up the hill last night in the storm."

"It's down the hill? And you brought a *car* up here?"

Okay, I definitely did not like him looking at me like I was stupid. That was my job. "Yeah. It did great up until the last turn. Where's your car?" I hadn't seen any vehicles parked in front of the cabin when I had arrived.

Chase raised his eyebrows. "My *truck* is parked in the garage."

He strode toward the window, flinging back the polyester curtain as he peered outside. My stomach lurched at the swirling snow. "We must have gotten close to ten inches last night, with more to come. It was below freezing all night."

"Yeah, I was aware of that," I said, stopping next to the doorway to pull on my boots.

He sighed as he moved toward the coat rack. "You'll probably need some muscle then."

"Matt's not here, so I'll just do it myself."

"Good one, pimple."

I smacked him hard against the chest.

"See? Blister's way better."

He reached for his coat before my words stopped him. "Thank you, but I really don't need your help. When I come back, I'd be happy to implement the no talking and ignore each other plan."

His body stilled. I opened the door, feeling his eyes on me. I stepped outside, closed the door, and immediately slipped on the black ice. If Chase heard my yelp of alarm, he wisely kept the door shut. Though I didn't look back to see, it wouldn't have surprised me to see him laughing at me from the window. The fall stunned my entire central nervous system and had me gasping for air for an excruciating ten seconds. The pain hit, shooting sharp jabs directly up my leg and back. A few minutes and a few choice words later, I was standing, gingerly making my way across the snow-covered black ice and onto the driveway; what was left of it anyway.

To my left was a mountainside forest, littered with trees that were now covered by ten inches of snow. To my right was a sharp drop off into who knows what. It was clouded over with fog, and with the mountains in the distance and the trees next to me, even with my sour mood at present, I couldn't fail to take notice of the beautiful winter wonderland before me. I almost wished Chase had come with me so he could see it himself. Almost.

At a bend in the road, I moved to step around what looked like the after-effect of an avalanche. A large pile of snow on my left felt like it went a mile high, as it lay against the mountainside.

Great. Avalanches. Now there was no doubt that, once I got my food and luggage, this would be my last excursion into nature before I left in a week. The snow crunched beneath my feet while I walked the trail, lost in thought.

I stopped short. I looked around and then back up toward the cabin. Where was my car? I knew I hadn't walked beyond this point last night. I remembered passing the Smokey the Bear sign in my car. It may have been the trigger for the downward spiral that led to thinking about Bigfoot. I looked around, confused. Had it slid off the side of the road? I moved carefully next to the cliff and peered over the edge. Fog and treetops were all that greeted me. I checked for tracks, but that proved useless as the snow had covered up any tracks that would have been made.

My confusion at this point began to ebb into full-blown panic mode.

Where was my car? Sure, it was just an old Corolla. It definitely had no business traversing up a mountainside during one of the biggest snowstorms to hit Idaho in twenty years, but it was all I had. What was I supposed to do? Besides, it had gotten me pretty close. I couldn't afford another car, and insurance wouldn't pay out enough to avoid a clunker. My breathing became shallow and sharp, piercing my throat in the cold. Could someone have stolen it? My eyes traveled back toward where the cabin sat, just behind the bend. I briefly wondered if Chase had moved it to play a prank.

No. It couldn't be Chase. He had been genuinely surprised to hear I had a car down the road.

Frustration welled up as tears in the corner of my eyes. "Stop it, Penny," I told myself, as I dabbed at my eye with my coat sleeve. There was really only one thing to do at this point, and part of me would rather die than grovel. I turned and stalked up the driveway once more, mourning the loss of my pajamas and boxes of probably very frozen bread, mac and cheese, and cereal, even more than my car. I hoped Chase brought more food than he thought, and I hoped he thought I was kidding about ignoring him.

Ha. Ha. What a kidder I was.

I rounded the bend, the cold really settling into my lungs at this point, giving the avalanche a wide berth before moving past.

Then something dawned on me. A bit slowly, but I'm only thankful it occurred to me before I did the walk of shame back to the cabin. With a sharp gasp, I whirled around and stared at the mound of snow piled on the roadway.

"No, no, no," I muttered, even as my head told me, yup; this is exactly what you think it is.

I approached the pile and gave it a kick with my foot. A small snow slide revealed a section of a black rubber tire. It took me ten minutes, approximately seventeen swear words, and a new winter coat of snow plastered to my body, before the side of my car was dusted off to the point where I could attempt to open the door.

That's exactly what it was; an attempt.

So much more swearing. This time it was encased with grunting, pulling, and jamming my big toe after an extremely frustrating kick to the car. I needed help. Although I knew Chase would help me, I couldn't stomach the thought of asking him after what I had just said to him.

A fine time to start being a feminist.

I admitted defeat a full half-hour after I set out on my journey. My next plan included slipping into the cabin, and nonchalantly slipping back out with a big jug of steaming hot water to pour over the car handle and seams of my door. It had to work. I would not be at Chase's mercy.

Thankfully, he was nowhere in sight when I re-entered the cabin. I rummaged through the kitchen cupboards before finding an old plastic pitcher. I ran the faucet for a minute before thick, hot steam filled the air. After filling it as full as I dared, bearing a treacherous journey back down the hill, I set off slowly, but anxiously, toward the door. I had just made it when Chase's voice made me pause.

"What are you doing?"

Dang it.

I casually turned toward him, not quite meeting his eyes, and said, "Just planning to enjoy a nice jug of hot water out on the porch."

He stared at me as though he were mentally counting backward in his head, before striding to the coat rack, jamming his arms through his heavy Carhartt coat, and pulling on his boots. He opened the door and motioned me ahead of him through the doorway. "Where's your car?"

I pointed down the road and followed a few careful paces behind his impatient stride, grunting every time the hot water sloshed on my body. The heat from the water seemed to evaporate instantly into ice on my hands. How cold was it?

Chase stopped abruptly as we came around the curve, and he took in the sight of my car. I must admit, even the second time seeing it, it looked really bad.

"Kiss it goodbye."

I stopped next to him, putting one of my frozen hands inside my pocket for warmth. "What? No way. I'm going to—"

"I know what you were going to do, but you can't. It's ten below out here. The second you pour the water on your car, it will freeze. Not to mention, probably ruin your car in the long run."

"But everything's in there. My food. My clothes." My flannel pajamas.

He walked closer to the vehicle and began working the handle, jiggling places all around, trying to get something to open, when the snow on top of the car from the avalanche was shaken loose just enough to send a shower of packed snow cascading toward us. More specifically, Chase. Within seconds, he was Chase no longer, but a puffy, frosted snowman with angry eyes. Well, I don't know if Chase can get angry, but they were definitely annoyed eyes.

I set the jug of warm water on the ground while I sheepishly helped to brush the snow off the back of his coat.

"If we do anything else to this car, the snow will fall down and cover the road, and then we'll both be stuck here until it melts. You'd better say goodbye to the car for now. And everything inside." He moved to stand closer to me, flinging his arm around my shoulder and pulling me in close before adding, "I guess your wildest dream came true. You get to cozy up next to me for a week."

"Great."

As two bundles of exasperation waddled back up to the cabin, I allowed his arm to remain around my shoulders, purely for the warmth it provided.

W e decided not to waste the hot water in the jug, although now it was more lukewarm, and dug through the cupboards for some hot chocolate. After filling our cups to the brim in semi-awkward silence, we both settled at the small kitchen table.

"So..." he began.

"Look," I started at the same time.

"You go first," I said.

He brushed his hand through his hair. "Okay, so logistically, this is where we're at; we have blankets and heat and water. So that's good."

I forced myself to hold his gaze while trying hard not to roll my eyes at his serious tone. The Marines really did a number on this guy.

"We have all the hot chocolate we can drink and some oatmeal, but other than that, we have to live off the food I brought, which I wasn't planning to have to share."

"Sorry."

He stopped speaking for a moment and looked at me—his brown eyes piercing into mine. "I don't mind sharing. What I meant was, I didn't pack much. I planned on eating a lot of fish."

I swallowed as I tore my gaze from his. "Fish?"

"I came here to ice fish all week."

My heart sunk. Although I knew if it came down to a matter of life and death, I would eat fish, but really, I would have to be almost dying. I gave him a cheerful smile; being literally at his mercy, after all. "Sounds great. What else did you bring with you?"

"Breakfast stuff. Eggs, a few potatoes, and lots of bacon. A loaf of bread, peanut butter...that kind of stuff."

"Great." My eyes lit up at the words *lots of bacon*. I could eat bacon.

He looked at me for a moment, a slight smile playing in the corner of his lips. "You don't like fish, Blister?"

Shoot. My cheerful response must have been over the top. I took a sip of my hot chocolate.

"I love it. And I appreciate you sharing, but my name is Penny."

"That's nice."

After a long silence, I couldn't help but add in forceful undertones, "And it *wasn't* a blister."

"I feel like the nickname is pretty generous, all things considered."

"Shut up."

He laughed, showing his smile. I'll admit, it was a great smile. It was all this big, sports-crazed, still stuck in high school, meathead had going for him. Of course, I would never admit that to him.

He drained the last of his hot chocolate and stood up, banging his mug on the table. "Well, suit up, Blister. It's time to go catch our lunch."

The color drained from my face. "What, now?"

"You heard me. Suit up."

I looked at him like he was stupid. "In what? All my clothes are in my car."

"You've got boots and a coat. And I just so happen to have an extra pair of overalls."

I clutched my warm mug tight in my hands. "Well, I'm sorry, but I need to write."

"You need to eat too, and if you think I'm going to let you just eat all my bacon, you're in for a disappointment."

"I wouldn't just eat the bacon. I'm a big fan of *all* breakfast food," I said, kindly.

He glared at me. "Well, I'm not big on handouts, but I am a fan of teaching a man to fish. Or in this case, woman. So, if you are planning on eating this week, you might want to go get dressed."

I glared at him. "I know how to fish." I didn't at all actually, but that didn't stop my chin from jutting out as I added boldly, "I love it."

"Really? Then this will be fun. We can exchange notes."

When I took my cup to the sink and headed toward my room, he poked his head out of his bedroom and flung a pair of overalls at me.

"Be ready to go in five minutes."

4

I had to roll the bottoms of the overalls three times, so they wouldn't drag on the ground. Thank goodness there were suspenders holding it all up because it would have never worked otherwise. My coat was tight around me as I zipped it up over the extra girth, leaving me feeling puffy, pudgy, and all-around unattractive. I waddled out of the room exactly seven minutes later, for the sole reason of annoying Chase. Although, the last two minutes of pacing my room, fully dressed, not allowing myself to be punctual probably hurt me much more than him.

Chase did a double take when I entered the living room, but beyond a slightly raised eyebrow, he wisely said nothing. He was dressed in thick, khaki overalls and a coat, with what looked like a sweatshirt underneath it all, as a hood stuck out from behind. He carried a backpack on one shoulder, a folded camp chair on his other shoulder, and in his hands he held two fishing poles.

"You brought two fishing poles, even though you weren't planning on a guest?"

He looked back at me as he reached the back door. "A real man always fishes with two poles."

"Why do *you* have two then?"

He opened the door and turned around to scowl at me while I glided past, the cold air knocking the breath from my lungs. "This ought to be fun. I'll bet an outdoors master like you could teach me a lot."

That shut me up.

Thankfully, Gina's cabin, although lacking in the fancy amenities department, had beautiful lakefront property. As we neared the ice-covered pond, my breath was once again taken away, but this time, not by the cold. Snow-covered pines completely encased the rounded lake. Fog from earlier this morning lingered on the tips of the trees, making me feel as if I had stepped into a snow globe. The ice steamed in spots, and all I could think was that I had somehow stumbled upon one of the most beautiful Christmas scenes my mind could have never conjured up. I had never felt so alive and so secluded at the same time. I noticed Chase seemed to study the picture before him with awe as well.

"Not bad, huh?"

I could only nod. "It feels like we're the only two people in the world."

Bite my Hallmark tongue.

I hadn't a clue where a hair-brained remark like that came from, especially given my current company and situation. I could only blame my loose tongue on the wonder of nature before my eyes, and the fact that I wrote romance novels for a living.

An arm came around me and settled onto my shoulders, pulling my stiff body into an awkward embrace. "Are you coming on to me right now, Penny?"

Blushing, I pushed him away. He chuckled and handed me a fishing pole, which felt as familiar to me as a nurse handing me a scalpel and telling me to start the surgery. Okay, I had obviously seen people fishing before, and I had the general idea of it all, but I had never once been. I had never even touched a pole that I could recall, and I definitely didn't know how to fling it into the water.

He motioned me forward. "Alright, let's go about ten or fifteen yards ahead and we'll drill a hole."

Drill? Like with a power tool?

"Sounds great," I said, confidently.

I stepped timidly onto the ice, bracing myself for my imminent death by hypothermia. Nothing. Not even a crack. I took another step, this time testing it gently with my full body weight. The ice groaned a bit, which stopped my heart, but the ground remained unmoved. I took another step, and another, slowly testing each area.

Chase had moved a few feet away, doing the same, testing each step carefully before putting his full weight on the ice. Encouraged, as I hadn't made a complete fool of myself yet, I pressed on. After another minute or two, Chase announced this would be a good spot. He set his chairs and pole down on the ground. I added mine to his and stood there awkwardly, praying he wouldn't ask me to do anything.

Chase pulled a cordless drill from his backpack, knelt down to the ice, and drilled a small hole. I watched with moderate interest. He was occupied and not looking at me, and I couldn't help but admire his confidence and, well, his hands. The way he gripped the drill with so much confidence. There was just something about a man who knows his way around a power tool. They were the kind of hands that could flip bacon, hunt a deer, and fix the carburetor all before lunch. Being in the great outdoors in the secluded setting, and suddenly, I was looking at Chase in a whole new light.

"Blister?"

And I was back.

"What?" He was laughing at me again. How long had he been calling me? How long had I been *ogling* him?

"You all right?"

"Yeah."

"Then hand me the ice chisel in the backpack, will you? Actually, there should be two."

I prayed with the strength of a thousand suns that I would know an ice chisel when I saw one.

Thankfully, there was just one option. Two, actually. I handed both to him. He only took one.

"The other one's for you. It's the most tedious part, so I know a real fisherman wouldn't trust just one person to do it. You know, to make sure it all goes right."

"Thanks." I avoided looking at his eyes because I strongly suspected he was laughing at me. I tried to hold the pole like I knew what I was doing, as I knelt down beside him. He took his pole and centered it above the hole and began moving it up and down, whittling away the ice, to create a bigger entrance. I mimicked his efforts and was relieved to find that it was not hard at all. Soon, we had a wide hole and we stopped. He stood and opened the camp chair, placing it next to me, but a foot or so away from the hole.

"You take this one. Sit here and cast your line and I'll go this way, twenty yards or so, and make another hole."

I made a big show of adjusting my chair and seat and getting comfortable until he was busy drilling a new hole. Then I held up my pole and stared at it.

I turned the handle thing on the right and the string dropped down a few inches. My eyes lit up. I had just cracked the code. I was so worried about trying to throw my line all graceful in front of the Mountain Man over there, that I hadn't realized I wouldn't have to throw it. I could just drop it in the hole, nice and easy.

I was feeling quite smug, which in hindsight, should have been a warning signal. My line was in the water, probably at least a couple feet, when a small, Styrofoam container landed on my lap.

I looked to Chase, questioningly.

"Surely an avid fisherman like yourself wouldn't forget to bait your hook."

I stared in secret horror at the innocent-looking container. I swallowed. "Of course not, I was just—testing the pole."

Testing the pole? Was that a fisherman's term? What was this game we were playing? We both knew I was far from being a fisherman, but I couldn't back down. Not to him. There was too much childhood angst for me to give him the satisfaction. It was that arrogant look he gave me all the time. Like he knew I was lying. Which, technically I was, but why did he always have to assume things about me?

I opened the lid quickly and efficiently. "I love baiting my hook."

Oh my gosh. STOP IT.

In the container, amid the top of the dark dirt, lay at least four, tangled worms. Who knew how many more were buried deep, waiting to pounce?

In case you didn't already figure, I was definitely more of an indoor girl.

He wasn't even trying to hold back his grin now. He was playing dirty. Trying to make a fool out of me. I gritted my teeth. Two could play that game.

I picked up a worm. It squirmed in my hand.

Oh, yuck. Yuck, yuck, yuck.

"So, how often do you go fishing?" I was quite impressed with how normal my voice sounded because my insides were fighting utter despair. I brought the tiny snake-like creature to my eye level. One step away from blowing my breakfast all over this redneck fishing hole. Do people really need fish so badly they would subject themselves to this? I wasn't even going to eat it. I'd be happy with rancid oatmeal for the rest of the week, and maybe just a *couple* of pieces of bacon. I glanced at Chase out of the corner of my eye and was dismayed that my attempt to draw him into conversation while I murdered a—well... either a bug, insect, or some sort of reptile— proved futile. Either way, instead of going back to his business and talking like a *normal*, nice human, he just stood there watching me, arms folded, and completely entertained.

"A few times a year is all."

The talking stilled as we both stared expectantly at the worm in my hand.

Summoned to the guillotine, I raised my head high and set my fishing pole on the ground. I had to do this. I slid my fingers along the fishing line until I held the hook. All romantic thoughts about the woods and this lake I had earlier, fled.

Nature was a cruel, dark place.

I put the hook next to the worm, took a deep breath, and—speared him.

And then I turned gracefully away and dry heaved for a solid ten seconds.

We caught three fish. Not we. I.
    Me.

As in, I caught three fish. Chase caught none. While I didn't sing, 'We are the Champions,' I definitely hummed the song as we packed up. Chase was quiet. A suspicious quiet. Almost as if he was suppressing a laugh, but beyond an occasional side-eye, I paid him no mind. I was on cloud nine. My first time fishing, I speared a disgusting worm four times and caught three fish. Maybe I was cut out for this wilderness life. It was only while gliding home that I was brought back down to earth with one perfectly timed comment. He had let me have my moment, but it was all a ruse.

"Well, that's great, you can eat your fish and I'll just eat my own food today since I didn't catch anything."

My heart dropped. "Oh no, I'm happy to share."

"No. I know how much you love fish, so go ahead and eat your catch today, I'll try again tomorrow."

I was going to starve on this trip.

"Doesn't it feel good to survive off the land?"

By this time, we had reached the cabin door. He opened the door and held it for me to walk in before him. I glanced up and found a challenging glint in his eyes, lurking behind the laughter. My heart had stooped so low, I couldn't even say anything as I passed through the threshold.

"And just think, now you get to skin and clean the fish for lunch."

That did it. I stopped, my shoulders drooped and sagging. The pole and camp chair I carried clattered to the floor as I turned back to face him. He had broken me.

"Okay, you win. I can't do this. I hate fish. I'd never even been fishing before but felt like I had to and...and I can't gut it and clean it. Please." It was pathetic. A new lowest of the low. And then he started clapping, slowly.

"Well, you lasted a lot longer than I thought you would."

"What?"

He cocked his head to one disbelieving side, as he leaned closer to me. "You put on a good show. And really, catching three fish when you're not trying to is pretty impressive."

"Please don't make me eat them."

He stared at me for a second, pondering. "I'll skin and clean the fish, and I'll show you how to cook it. But you have to eat it, I'm not letting you eat all my food in two days' time."

I was about to complain but wisely refrained. This was Survivor, and Chase Riley was my food source. Well, I probably wouldn't eat him if it came to that, but he was the one who could provide me with food. It pained me to even think those thoughts.

"Deal," I said, as I moved to my room. Maybe I could try the old clothespin on the nose trick. Or maybe, the fish would taste better caught fresh in the mountains.

For the record. They did not taste better.

Two nights later, I opened my door a tiny crack and peeked out into the hallway. The clock on my phone said 1 am. The house was pitch black and all signs pointed to Chase being in his bed, asleep. I shot past the doorway like a graceful gazelle and bounded into the bathroom, shutting the door gently. With the heater on in my room, there was no need or desire to sleep in my jeans, which meant I wore my tank top and the most unattractive, gray panties I owned. Every stitch of my rear end was completely covered, and then some. I was not proud of this, but I was supposed to be alone in a cabin by myself for a week, so I packed a week's worth. Too bad the other six days of panties sat frozen and stuck in my car. But no matter, earlier that night, I washed them in the sink and left them on the floor heater in my room to dry. It had only taken them about fifteen minutes.

I finished up my business and washed my hands before yanking open the door.

A rumpled, bed-headed Chase stood just outside the door, a dazed look on his face and a hand, half-raised as he squinted against the harsh bathroom light. He wore a pair of basketball shorts with no shirt and I felt annoyed at the sight of his relaxed, comfortable clothing. Or lack thereof. As his eyes adjusted to the light, my skin prickled while his gaze slid over me. Shoot. I didn't care about Chase at all, but if I were married, I wouldn't even show my husband this underwear. I'd burn it. They were not for public viewing. My right hand shot out as my fingers fumbled along the bathroom wall. Two bottles clanged to the floor in my desperate search for the light switch. Finally, the light switched off.

I could feel the heat from his body as we stood facing each other.

"Well, thanks for at least putting on some shorts, Blister."

"Shut up."

"Or should I say, Grandma?"

"Shut up," I said again, as I brushed past him, not able to resist jamming my shoulder into his as I turned toward my room.

I slammed my door to the sound of him chuckling.

5

When I walked into the living room the next morning, prepared to ignore Chase for the entire day, I stopped in my tracks. Scattered across the couches and the backs of chairs were clothes. Men's clothes. My eyes alighted first on a pair of gray sweats. They would be too big for me, but they looked like heaven. I forced my eyes to keep moving. A week's worth of t-shirts, a couple of long-sleeved undershirts, a package of boxer briefs, a hooded sweatshirt, and a pile of men's crew socks, piled high on a couch cushion. Chase sat relaxing on the lounge chair, watching me.

"Laundry day?"

He smiled. "Possibly."

My eyes widened. Could he be intending to share some of his clothes? My eyes flicked involuntarily to his sweatpants, looking very under-appreciated. Could it be that Chase Riley had finally grown a compassionate heart?

"It came to my attention last night that you are in need of some clothes, and possibly some new underwear that wasn't designed in 1945."

I glared at him. "Let me remind you that I was supposed to be here alone."

"After what I saw last night, the *alone* part doesn't shock me." His lazy grin did nothing to stop the sharp blow of daggers suddenly stabbing against my chest at his words.

"She looks like my dog, but not as hot."

Words. Those stupid, meaningless words from long ago flew into my thoughts. Dang it. I didn't care about that. Not anymore. Why was this happening? Moisture filled my eyes against my will. I quickly turned my back to Chase, hoping he didn't notice. I wasn't quick enough.

"Hey."

Movement from behind me had me wiping my eyes quickly before he grabbed my shoulder and turned me to face him.

I smiled brightly up at him and said, "I'm fine. Something's in my...eye."

"Both of them?"

I couldn't think of anything to say, so I just wiped at my eyes once more, while Chase stared on, looking miserable. I probably would have laughed if it wasn't so awkward.

"I shouldn't have said that, I..." He gazed uneasily at me as he brushed a hand through his hair. "I was just messing with you."

"I know."

"I didn't mean it." For his part, Chase did look troubled. I just felt stupid for making such a scene. It was ridiculous that the tiniest thing from eighth grade, almost fifteen years ago, had caused such a reaction. Then, as if he couldn't take the friction in the air between us either, he added, "Your granny underwear looked great."

I smacked him across the chest, both of us now fighting smiles. The tension in the room began to evaporate. Perfect. We could laugh about it. That, I could handle. Concerned, brown, doe eyes staring into mine was something else entirely. A bridge we definitely hadn't crossed.

Motioning around the room with my head, I asked, "So do I have to arm wrestle you for these or something?"

"I was thinking we could play for them."

"Play for them?" My interest level heightened considerably.

He had a gleam in his eyes that should have scared me. "Texas Hold 'Em, just like we used to. Nothing fancy. We play until the clothes run out. Winner of each game gets to pick an article of clothing to use the rest of the week."

"Kind of like, reverse strip poker."

"Yup. Although if you're more comfortable with regular strip poker, that would be fine with me."

"Ha."

My eyes drifted ravenously towards the gray sweatpants flung across the back of the chair. A Cowboys sweatshirt. The boxer briefs.

He held up a hand. "A few words about the underwear."

I raised my eyebrows.

"I just grabbed this new pack at the store on the way to the cabin a couple of days ago. Only *one* pair is up for grabs, I just kept them in the package so you'd believe me that they were brand new."

A pair of his boxers meant I could have an alternate. Something to wear at night while I washed and dried my pair. Drying my pair on the heater hadn't been bad, but this meant I wouldn't be trapped in my room while they dried. Men's underwear or not, I could definitely make them work.

"What do you say, Blister? You want to play?"

"How about we just cut to the chase and you just let me borrow some of this stuff right now?"

He furrowed his brow as if this were the craziest idea, goading me. "What? No handouts here, Blister. In my house, you gotta earn 'em."

"It's not your house."

One corner of his mouth quirked upward. "Fine. *Our* house."

My face flushed with his insinuation. While my heart banged around in my chest, I swallowed and pushed the conversation forward. "What are we playing with?"

He motioned to the table, toward a big jar of coins. "Found it in the dresser in my room."

I bit my lip, unsuccessfully trying to keep myself from smiling. Walking over toward the table, I snatched the deck of cards out of his hands. "I'm dealing."

He slapped his hands together with exaggerated gusto as we set ourselves up at the table.

Just like old times, minus the six other people at the table who acted as a buffer between me and Chase. This should be fun.

I'd be lying if I said I didn't enjoy a good poker game. The last time Chase and I had played poker together was in high school, with my brother Matt and their friends. It had become a ritual for us. The weekend football parties at our house would usually end with a poker game or two, full of teasing and good-natured ribbing. Not being a sports fan, but desperate to remain close to my brother, I had been surprised at how much I enjoyed poker, and honestly, I had been pretty good.

It was pure luck, but I had a bit of a knack for reading people. It was the writer in me. I was always watching for clues in the faces at the table to see just what their hands might hold. I had begun to get a reputation among the guys as the one to beat. I left many tables with the night's winnings, more often than not. The only person to really give me a run for my money was Chase Riley.

We slipped easily into the game, picking up as naturally as if we'd just played last week. Only this time, instead of lunch money, old boy clothes were the prize. A thick and soft sweatshirt, sweatpants, socks, t-shirts, basketball shorts, and even boxer briefs. Nothing had ever looked better to me. My body could feel the clothes wrapped around me, cocooning me in warmth and comfort; but first, I needed to win.

"Alright, Blister," he began, while he shuffled the worn deck of cards, "You remember how to play?"

"Just like riding a bike."

His head shot upward. "Like the bike ride where you biffed it, coming in hot to the little league game when we were kids?"

I snorted out a laugh before I could stop myself. A quick glance at Chase showed he was pleased with his efforts to tease me. Luckily, the crash and burn on my bike had been more crash and less burn, but I had unfortunately taken out several little leaguers at the expense of my negligence.

"Should we make this interesting?" Chase sat poised, with the cards in his hands about ready to deal, his eyes on me.

I motioned to the clothes strewn about the room. "I thought we already were."

He shook his head. "We have something for the winner, but nothing for the loser."

My eyes narrowed. "*If* I happen to lose, I have to keep wearing my uncomfortable work clothes. That seems pretty horrible to me."

He shook his head. "Nah. You *will* lose, and I'd really like somebody on dish duty. Or a back rub."

I glanced over to the sink full of dishes. Correction...the sink full of *Chase's* dishes. The small cabin didn't have a dishwasher, and while I had gotten in the habit of washing my plate and cup after each use, Chase had not.

"No way. They're all your dishes. Just wash them after you're done using them."

He sighed, leaning back on his chair, stretching his arms in the air. "I'm just always so tired after slaving away, cooking us both breakfast and dinner."

"No." I kept my eyes diligently averted from the sliver of muscly torso that showed when his shirt rode up as he stretched. Nope. I wasn't tempted to look *at all,* and I kept my eyes zeroed in on him *almost* the entire time. Yup, just call me 'no peek Penny.' Yeah, the back rub thing was out of the question.

He smiled, like a cat who had a mouse in his paws. "It's either dish duty or a twenty-minute back massage every time one of us loses, or I take my clothes and walk away right now."

If I reached across the table right at that moment, I wondered if I could wrap my hands around his neck and squeeze before he realized what I was doing? Memories of playing games and doing deals on Friday nights came roaring back to me. I had lost many things at his demand. Of course, he had lost several things to me as well, but I knew he wouldn't give up until I relented.

"Fine. Dish duty for the loser."

He smiled and began dealing out the cards. "What a great idea."

He won the first hand with a pair of sevens.

He stood and made a big show of perusing the items as if he were on some award show.

"Just pick one," I ordered. The longer he stood there, the more nervous I was that his sweatpants and sweatshirt would be taken. Even though I needed the underwear, I really wanted some loungewear. A stiff work blouse and tight jeans did not a cozy cabin make.

As if knowing the exact thing he could do to annoy me, he picked up his sweatpants and examined them carefully. Rubbing the soft material against his face in a ridiculous manner, and with such exaggerated moaning sounds, it forced me to hurl at him the only thing I could find within reach, the TV remote. He laughed as it bounced off his shoulder. He tossed the pants back on the chair and grabbed his basketball shorts off the couch.

"I'm dealing," I said as he sat back down, his shorts draped over his shoulder.

"Should we take a quick break so you can get a head start on those dishes?" He leaned back in his chair, his arms folded behind his head, looking very pleased with himself. Visions of myself kicking the chair out from under him were my only solace as I shuffled the cards.

He won the second game. Okay, this was starting to get annoying. He picked one of the two shirts he had on display. I jumped when his hands began rubbing my shoulders, firm and in just the right spot. Though my first inclination was to push him away, I allowed myself just a second or two of pure, heated bliss. Another point for those sexy man hands.

"Sure you don't want to trade for a back massage?" He whispered in my ear, his breath tickling the length of my spine. "I'm sure you'll take this next game."

Nope. Nope. Nope. I shook him off while he chuckled and sat back down. He was playing dirty now.

The third and fourth games, he won.

The fifth game; dirty rotten snake.

The sixth game; swear words.

Utter despair clawed at my emotions. I was *so* close. So close. This poker bet was as close to kindness as Chase would ever be inclined to offer me, and I had nothing to show for it. Why couldn't the cards be reasonable tonight? He had taken a pair of socks, his sweatshirt, both of his long-sleeve undershirts, and was now opening the pack of underwear. I still had nothing.

"I'm just going to donate this pair of underwear to you," he said, ripping the package open and tossing me a pair of black boxer briefs. "I just feel like it would be best for all involved."

To my utter shame and embarrassment, I couldn't even pretend not to want them. I needed them. I clutched the underwear to my chest gratefully, as two pairs of socks smacked me in the head.

"Why don't you just give me some of the other stuff too?" I asked, already knowing his sick and twisted answer.

"Because this is too fun."

He came back over to the table and sat down. He stared at me. I stared back, and a smile began curling at his lips.

"Okay," he said. "Last game."

We both eyed the sweatpants.

"Deal the cards," I said. For the freaking love, I had to win. For all womanhood and mankind in general. For every woman who had ever lost to a conceited, arrogant, attractive jerk, I had to win.

In the end, however, I lost. I was sitting much worse than I was before we started the blasted game. I still had no sweatpants, and I would be doing dishes all week. Chase couldn't even bring himself to tease me about losing seven games in a row, and the idea that Chase could possibly be feeling sorry for me made it a thousand times worse.

"Double or nothing."

I thought I dreamed his words for a moment. His hand slipped into mine and he tugged it toward him, forcing me to lift my defeated head off my arms and meet his eyes. I fully expected smugness, but instead, I found... sweetness? No, that couldn't be right.

"What?"

"Double or nothing." That's what I thought he said. There had to be a catch.

"What's the terms?" I asked, warily pulling my hand out of his grasp.

"One more game. This time we play Five Card Draw. If you win, you can pick two of my things."

My eyes narrowed. "And if you win?"

"I get a back massage *and* you clean and cook our dinner."

I dropped my head back onto my arms on the table, ignoring him. Okay, so he obviously wasn't feeling as sorry for me as I had imagined. Out of the whole morning, all I had received were a lousy pair of boxer briefs and two pairs of socks, already on my feet. Both had been a mercy donation. I had nothing to lose. When I let myself imagine massaging his back, my stomach flipped over before I refused to think about it anymore.

"I mean, seven in a row...odds are probably in your favor," he baited.

When I still refused to move, he added, "I'll just have a hard time sleeping at night, tucked away in all these clothes..."

"Deal 'em."

"You serious?" He nudged my foot under the table.

I looked up at him and nodded. "Deal the cards."

"You remember that I said a thirty-minute back rub, and cooking dinner was on the line."

"Ten minutes."

"Twenty."

"Fifteen."

"Deal."

"And I prefer my salmon cut thin with a crispy skin on top. A little lemon juice on the side."

"And I prefer you as a seventh-grader when you were too cool to talk to me."

"Ew. You prefer me as a seventh-grader?"

"Shut up." I kicked him under the table and turned my face away to hide the evidence of my smile.

He smiled as he dealt the cards. I bit my lip, holding off the grin clambering to break free. I waited until all five cards were dealt and in front of me before I drew them into my hand. My breath stilled as I immediately pulled a pair of sevens and two fives. A single Jack of hearts finished out my hand. I tamped down my excitement. Though they weren't high cards, they were pairs, and better than anything I had been given in our last seven games.

Chase quietly studied his hand for a minute. "How many are you trading?"

I shoved the down-facing Jack toward him, mustering up an air of superiority. "One."

He stared at me for a long moment, his eyebrow cocked. "You bluffing or playing, Blister?"

"I guess you'll find out."

A rueful grin appeared as he took my card and handed me another from the top. He looked at his cards once more, before exchanging three cards for himself.

"Three, wow," I muttered, purely working to get under his skin.

Again, that smile. My own smile, once again, threatened to break across my face, but then I pinched myself, forcing myself to remember just what was at stake. To give myself further encouragement, I glanced at the thick, comfortable cotton sweats dangling on the back of his chair. He wasn't even using them. He just kept them there to make me miserable. For a second, I wondered how quickly I could snatch the pants, run to my room and lock the door before he could catch me. Then I remembered he played football and I frequently played a game I liked to call, 'I'm not athletic and I fall down a lot.'

"You're up, Blister. What's your bet?"

I stared at my coins. Forty-six cents in pennies and nickels remained, and a button, which we had deemed worth a penny. Win or lose, I had no other option but to play this out. And I had to sell it, hard.

Since we were only betting once, I pushed my whole stack to the middle of the table. A low whistle met my ears before he added the same amount from his mountain of coins across the table. "I guess I can spare a couple quarters."

"Shut up." I shook my head, my smile finally breaking free.

Sitting up in my chair, I fidgeted in my seat, holding my breath, as if I were trying hard to contain my excitement. Chase watched me carefully.

A smile crawled across his face as he shook his head. "Nice try, Blister."

"What?"

"You're a lot of things, but I can spot when you're bluffing a mile away."

I held strong. "Well, this should be fun then."

"This will be fun. My back's been feeling a little sore today."

We sat for a moment, staring at each other, hard and challenging, until it became something different entirely, both of us fighting back smiles. But then he blinked, and his face softened the tiniest bit. His eyes were still on mine, but the glint had disappeared, and in its place was something that had my heart beating faster. I cleared my throat and shifted back in my seat, breaking our eye contact, and also breaking the mood, or whatever that was.

"Let's see 'em."

My eyes shot to his. "What?"

He looked at me and said slowly, "The cards. Show 'em."

"Oh. Right." I drew it out, placing each of my cards on the table slowly, starting with my pair of fives, then my sevens. I held off a bit, building up the anticipation. The last card I had drawn had been a ten of spades, not helpful in the least. Now, I could only hope and pray that he had nothing in that hand of his.

"Ouch," he said. "Bet you were really hoping for a full house, huh?"

I smiled. "Nah. I'm happy to beat you with two pairs."

"What was our bet again?"

"Quit stalling and play your cards."

He sighed. He laid down a three of spades. Then a four of spades. His next card was a five of spades. My heart sunk. Two more cards in a row and he would have a straight flush. He laid down a six of spades. My breath caught. No way. He could *not* be this lucky. I shot my eyes up to meet his, daring to hope. Then he smiled at me and tossed his card toward the middle of the table. I stared at the jack for several seconds before I realized what it meant.

I had won.

I screeched as I leaped from the table, my hands shooting straight into the air as I hopped around in a ridiculous victory dance. The moves from my high school poker night victory days came back to me in a rush.

The gray sweatpants hit me in the face. "Alright, settle down, hotshot. What's your other pick?"

"How'd you know I wanted these?"

"The drool running down your face was a dead giveaway."

"Shut it."

"What's your next pick? You better hurry, my offer only lasts for another thirty seconds."

"Sweatshirt," I said, as I picked it up, put it on, and then immediately wished I hadn't. It smelled like outdoors and pine trees, maybe a little sweat and something sweeter, the faint smell of cologne or something. I wanted to breathe that air forever.

"Oh, this smells good."

His eyes lit up and I realized my error. I had said those words out loud. I couldn't help it; my senses had been completely clouded over with amazing man smells.

He grinned, the hunter zeroing in on the stunned deer in his headlights. "That's just the imitation. You should try the real thing sometime."

I didn't appreciate the lurch in my stomach or the way the goosebumps flushed all along my arms. I had to get out of there. He was much too attractive for his own good, and for my own good.

"For now, I'll be good with just this," I said, wrapping my arms around my body.

"For now."

I looked at him in surprise. He just smiled. I'm not sure what scared me more, the thought that trying the real thing sounded intriguing, or the fact that there was no teasing gleam in his eye when he said it.

6

The next day I hid in my room for most of the morning.

I had things to do; important things. Things that had been put off because of a certain someone demanding all my time fishing, playing poker, watching old John Wayne movies in the evening, giving me clothes, and giving me food. Not to mention, giving me looks that Chase Riley should definitely not be giving me. Looks that made my hands feel awkward and my arms feel ten feet long.

The quiet was good because at the rate I was currently writing, I'd have my book published in about five years. I spent the morning touching up a few scenes, all the while plotting a new romance book. Cue palm to the face. Something about two strangers who found themselves trapped in a cabin for a week. Not related to my present predicament at ALL. It had been done before, plenty of times, but not by me. Now, with insider information, I felt I could do a story like that some romantic justice. Of course, I'd really have to rouse my imagination for the romance part.

Except that was a lie.

I was learning how extremely *not difficult* it was to imagine romance with someone when you were literally bathed in their magnificent boy scent, by way of a pair of extremely comfortable sweatpants and shirt. It all felt so...intimate, in the most innocent way possible. I was wearing his unwashed clothes that were basically ripped straight from his rock-hard body and given to me, (after a knock-down, drag-out poker game) and I found myself liking it.

Hence, the hiding.

I made it until exactly 10:30 am before I emerged from my hideout. Hey, a girl's got to eat. Chase seemed almost relieved when he saw me enter the kitchen. He was sprawled on the couch, reading an old Louis L'Amour western, but at my approach, he flung it behind him and stood up with a flourish. My mouth dropped open as the book crashed to the floor.

"*That* is a book," I spat, horrified.

At my death glare, he slowly raised his hands in surrender, as he bent to pick up the discarded book off the floor and placed it on the coffee table.

"Thank you." I turned my attention to the cupboard and began rummaging through it, even though I knew there would be no surprises. A girl could dream, right?

"The power's out. I saved you a couple pieces of bacon in the fridge."

His voice came from behind me, though not as far away as he had been before. I closed the cupboard and turned back to look at him. He leaned casually against the countertop in the kitchen, with his hands in the pockets of his basketball shorts. His rumpled brown hair stuck out from beneath a baseball hat. He looked effortlessly cool and dangerously...hot. Did I mention he just told me he saved me some bacon? I swallowed and licked my lips, then I realized what I just did and looked away, tucking a piece of stray hair behind my ear.

"Thanks," I said as I edged in a daze toward the fridge. I needed to keep moving to get away from his gaze, but his eyes followed me. How did I know that when I wouldn't look at him directly? Goosebumps broke out across my body, across my arms, my neck, my legs, everywhere his brown eyes touched. That was the only explanation. I opened the fridge to find an entire plate full of food waiting for me—

two fried eggs, diced homemade hash browns, and three large pieces of bacon.

"When the power comes back on, you can heat the whole plate up but for now, cold bacon isn't anything to sneeze at."

The voice came right behind my ear, causing me to jump and step back in surprise, right into a very warm body. I froze. He chuckled lightly as he placed his hands on my shoulder, moving me gently to the side. He reached into the fridge, grabbed the bacon pieces off the plate, and handed them to me.

"You're a little jumpy this morning. Having a man cook you some bacon must really do it for you."

It did. It *really* did, but I needed to get control of myself before I did something I would regret—like kiss the annoyingly adorable smirk off Chase's face. I took the bacon he offered and tried to gather up my pride that was spilled all over the floor.

"It does. Let me know when a man shows up."

His eyes narrowed, even as the corners of his mouth lifted. "You wanna play?"

My smirk disappeared. What now?

He looked as if he wanted to laugh at my reaction, but instead motioned to the table in the corner. A torn and well-loved red and black checkers game, probably older than both of us combined, sat innocently on top.

I smiled, shaking my head slightly. "What happened to the whole 'ignoring each other' plan?"

He smiled back. For about five whole seconds he stood, not speaking, but staring into my eyes, while fire raced up my body. "I don't think that was ever in the cards for us." His voice sounded low and gravelly to my ears, setting my entire body ablaze.

Well, I suppose I could play *one* game.

ONE game. Then it was back to my room. I had things to do that included staying far away from laughing eyes, goosebumps, and a warm body.

"Are you sure you can handle it? Playing games didn't work out so well for you yesterday." I attempted a smirk, trying to bring us back to where I was comfortable. A place full of sarcasm and boundaries.

His eyes skimmed over my body, taking in his sweatshirt that hung past my hips and his sweatpants that dragged on the floor when I walked. A small smile lit across his face. "Oh, I think it worked out pretty well for me."

And I'm back. My face flushed with heat and I debated, once again, the merits of staying in this room with the tension crackling between us. My body, however, had other plans and was apparently *all in*, so I pulled back the chair nearest the wall and sat at the table before my over-active mind could persuade me otherwise. Chase pulled out the chair across from me and sat down.

"Hey, 1985 called and they want their Checkers game back," I said, feigning nonchalance, as I lined up the red chips on my side of the board.

He smirked but said nothing, his eyes intense as he stared at the board. Once his chips were in place, he moved one of his black chips forward.

"Hey, ladies first."

He looked around the room. "Let me know if you find one."

A breath of relief escaped out of me before I could stop it. I could handle *that*, the back and forth, the sarcasm, the satisfaction of hearing his groan when I kicked him under the table. I made my move.

"So, why are you here this close to Christmas? Where's your family?" I asked him, while his eyes flicked across the board in calculated measure. It might be a late night of writing if my day was going to be wrapped up in Checkers.

"My parents are visiting my brother and his family in North Carolina for Christmas. I'm leaving here on Christmas Day and then I'll hang out with my older sister's family in Eugene later that day."

He made his next move and looked at me. "You?"

He had one of my chips trapped already. I ignored it and moved a chip that was still safe. "Same. My parents are in London visiting my sister and her family. Matt and Gina are meeting me up here on Christmas Day."

"You didn't want to be a third wheel either, then?"

I barked out a laugh. "Oh, I'm definitely still a third wheel, but only for one day, not a whole week."

He shook his head as he jumped over two of my red chips. "Are you even going to try to make this a game?"

His capture of my two reds left three of his black chips vulnerable. I grinned as I took all three with a flourish. "I believe I'm ahead, Riley."

"Typical civilian. Never looking at the long game." He perused the board, the line in his forehead creasing.

"So, are you still in the Marines? Or what do you do now?" It felt strange to be asking normal, human-type questions to Chase while we each moved pieces across the board. The other alternative, which seemed to be heat-induced stares and teasing grins, left me feeling muddy and confused, so the questions seemed safer.

"No. During my eight-year run with them, I went to school full time and got a master's degree in Construction management, and now I own my own company in Boise."

"Building houses?"

"Usually. Some commercial buildings, but my bread and butter comes from building starter homes."

Chase turned his baseball hat backward as he leaned forward, examining the board. Great. That didn't help him look hotter *at all*.

"So, you got a boyfriend?"

Well, that was one question I hadn't been anticipating. Too bad I had been taking a large gulp of water and choked. Nothing sprayed out or anything like that, it just went down the wrong pipe. I sat, coughing for a few long moments, while Chase watched me, amused. He couldn't even let me be embarrassed in peace.

"No. You?" Deflection. My best defense.

"Boyfriend? No."

I nudged him under the table again. "Girlfriend?"

"No. Should we play the question game?"

My stomach tightened. "No."

He grinned. "Yes."

"Let's just play this super exciting game of Checkers. I'm literally on pins and needles awaiting your next move." If he sensed my sarcasm, he didn't react and went on perusing the board as if he had nothing but time. Well, I guess that was probably pretty accurate. He looked up and I met his eyes across the table, both of us trying not to smile. I shook my head slightly, breaking eye contact and giving my attention to the fascinating wall just past his head.

Suddenly, something small and gray darted around the corner and scurried toward the living room, burying itself behind the rack of coats by the front door. Now, I hate to be that cliché girl, you know, the one who's terrified of mice and screams and points and jumps on the table. But...surprise...it's me. I'm most definitely *that* girl.

I screeched, jumping up from my seat to the table, all within an impressive two seconds' time. At my screams, Chase shot out of his seat, his chair sliding away behind him as he whirled around, no doubt looking for some sort of intruder. When he saw nothing, he circled back around to me and raised his arms in question.

"What?"

My mouth gaped open, but I kept my eyes fixed on the spot where I had last seen the rodent. I pointed toward the door. "Mouse."

Chase swore and before I could blink, the checkers game went flying and he hoisted himself up on his knees next to me on the—way too small for two adults to be kneeling on—table. His arm settled around my shoulders as he pulled me into him, his eagle eyes trained on the spot by the door.

"Are you *kidding* me?" I pulled myself out of his grasp. "*You're* the army guy!"

He was laughing when he turned to look at me. "Marine."

"Whatever. Get over there and get him!"

He held his hands up. "I don't do mice."

I gaped at him. "No, *I* don't do mice. *You* are the guy. *You* do the mice."

"And let you miss out on the opportunity to crush a stereotype?"

Feeling frantic at the idea of a disgusting rodent occupying the same space as me, I attempted to push him off the table. He grabbed my hands and held me at bay, laughing as he warded me off. I glanced across the room toward the door only to see the mouse dart toward the kitchen.

I screamed. Chase turned in time to see the mouse charge toward us and pulled us both up so we were standing on the table, hands clutched together and bent over, laughing hysterically. The kind of laughs where nothing comes out, we are just wheezing and sucking in air. When I had calmed down enough to feel his grasp on my hand, I pulled my hand from his and pushed my hair out of my face —if only to give my hands something else to do.

"Where did he go?"

"He took a hard right down the hallway, headed straight for your room," Chase said.

I gasped and turned back around, only to smack him on the stomach when I saw he was joking.

"I'm kidding. I'm pretty sure he's behind the back-door curtain."

I shifted, eyeing the back door carefully, searching for signs of the mouse. "Okay, it's time to be a hero, soldier." I nudged Chase and motioned for him to step down.

He only smiled and sat down on the table, pulling me down next to him, our feet dangling dangerously close to the ground. The heat from his body radiated from him. I really needed to move. I needed to get away from this proximity to him, but...you know...mouse.

"To be honest, I'm not sure where he is now. I was laughing too hard to take note," Chase said, squinting as he meticulously scanned the kitchen.

My heart sunk to a new low. He could be anywhere. I hope Chase made a good pillow because I guess that meant I wasn't leaving the table for the night. I forced myself to stop thinking about using Chase as a pillow, and instead, I pleaded in the most pathetic voice I could muster. "Please just go find it and kill it."

"Just face it. He's a part of our family now. What should we name him? Harold?" Chase asked, nudging me with his shoulder. Which, if

I had to guess, was exactly three millimeters from mine. So much for space.

I smiled in spite of myself. "Sure. Harold, it is."

"I don't do mice because they are disgusting, disease-carrying rodents of grossness. Why don't *you* do mice?" I asked him, half-debating over whether or not I should lean my head on his shoulder. It happened to be just the exact height of a shoulder my head needed. Suddenly, I felt very tired. I was nothing if not a walking contradiction.

"I had a *bad* experience." He drew out the word 'bad,' while his tone of voice sounded as though his memories had drifted to somewhere long ago.

I looked at him, waiting for him to add more. Nothing came. "What happened?"

"Nope. Not going back there. Just know, it was enough to make me completely comfortable jumping on the table like a little girl."

We sat there in dejected silence before Chase reached behind him, grabbing a handful of checkers pieces that hadn't flown off the table in all the crazy. He threw a black circle toward the front door. It clattered to the floor with an unimpressive force.

"What are you doing?" I asked.

"I'll feel better once I know where he's at. I found a sack full of traps in the laundry room earlier that we can set if we know where he is."

I picked up a checkers piece and threw one towards the kitchen. We waited, our ears perked for signs of life, before Chase threw another, this time toward the living room. A few long moments passed between us, as we sat in companionable silence, you know, trying to coax a mouse out of its hiding place.

"So, what kind of books do you write?"

I made a face, though he didn't see it. Looks like we were going to play the question game after all. I threw another checker. "I write books for women."

"For women, huh? The kind that are down that one aisle in the grocery store with the half-naked men on the cover?"

"What grocery store are you shopping at?" I threw a chip at his face. He laughed and swatted it away with quick, athletic prowess.

"Violent reaction alert. I think I got one right." He laughed, as my cheeks grew ruddy.

"No. I don't write those books. My books are women's fiction. And yes, they do have a bit of romance in them, but they are nothing like those books. Nobody is ever naked." Okay, the last part was true, but the 'bit' of romance part is stretching it a tad. The romance is definitely the main plot. I can't help it, I was born a hopeless romantic.

He laughed. "So is this week just feeding a flame for you, us all cozied up together in a mountain cabin?" His eyes grew wide as he asked, "Will I be in your next book?"

I opened my mouth only to close it again, thrown off balance for a moment. Did he somehow get a hold of my computer while I was showering or something? Denial. Denial. Denial.

"Ha. No way. I still can't believe that out of everyone in the world, I got trapped in this cabin with Chase Riley." I smirked at him. "It's a cruel world."

He just kept grinning at me as if he knew. My eyes narrowed—if he broke into my computer and saw my latest plot outline, I was going to kill him. After I hid in my room for the rest of the week. I mean, assuming I ever got off this table, of course.

"Why don't you have a girlfriend?" Perhaps that wasn't the most tactful transition, but I felt desperate to change the subject. Talking to close friends about what I write was hard enough, talking to Chase Riley was impossible. "I mean, I understand perfectly why you wouldn't, but looks can be deceiving for some."

Crap. I heard it. It was out of my mouth before I could stop it.

His eyes lit up as a lazy smile emerged across his face. "What are you saying?"

I wiped my sweaty palms on my sweatpants. *His* sweatpants. Ugh. Things were starting to feel confusing. My heart started to pound, even while I tried to play it cool. "You know what I meant."

"I do now."

"Just answer the question."

His smile finally faded, and he threw another checkers piece. "I've had girlfriends in the past, but nobody ever stuck. Simple as that."

"Was there a shortage of blonde cheerleaders?" My mind drifted to several cheerleaders, all of them blonde, that he had dated throughout high school. Not that I was keeping track, but Eugene was a small town.

"If I still wanted a blonde cheerleader, I'd be with one now."

I folded my arms, leaning forward on the table. "So many women throwing themselves at you, is that it?"

"Nah. But there is one playing hard to get."

I stopped breathing. The tension once again found its way into the room between us—crackling. I stared straight ahead, refusing to look at him, even as I could feel his stare burning a hole into the side of my head. The head that was currently spinning. What world did we land in? Was Chase Riley making a pass at me? At me? Of course not. I was the only thing for miles around, with female parts, trapped in a cabin with him. That's all it was.

She looks like my dog but not as hot. Yeah, and I'd do well to remember that.

I took a deep breath and exhaled, trying to move the air between us. "What do you want in a woman then? Enlighten me."

He blatantly looked at me, then his eyes roamed around my face, just long enough for my heart to start pounding. My breath hitched before he said, "Next question. How about you, Blister? Twenty-eight years old. I would have thought you'd be married with four kids and a minivan right about now."

My heart plummeted. That is why conversations with him were impossible; they left me feeling weird and unsettled, with my emotions all over the place. His question cut me deep, but I refused to show it. There had been a time I had thought so as well.

"I've had boyfriends in the past, but nobody ever stuck. Simple as that." He smiled at me when I threw his words back at him. All of a sudden, I realized how close we sat to each other. The sides of our bodies were practically one. If I moved one tiny finger, our hands would be touching. Why was he still looking at me? His eyes dropped to my lips and suddenly, I needed to get off the table. Mice or no mice. I took a small breath of courage before I leaped from the table and dashed toward the hallway.

"I'll grab the traps. You set them up."

"Hey, get back here, I didn't make that deal!"

"It's only fair," I shouted from the laundry room. I found the sack of traps Chase had mentioned and ran back toward him. I flung the bag onto the table next to him.

"What are you so scared of, Penny?" he asked, his hands flung out wide as he looked at me. My breath hitched at the sound of my real name from his lips, and I held his gaze for about three seconds too long.

"Mice," I said, turning to bolt down the hallway. Even when he called down the hallway after me, I refused to look back. I retreated as quickly as I could to my room, away from Chase, his eyes, and his hotness, and wrote a couple of chapters for my new book—about two people snowed in at a cabin.

I was in trouble.

———

Somewhere in the middle of the night, a loud snap sounded. And just like that, Harold was gone.

———

The next morning, I sequestered myself in my room once again, trying to write. For some reason, my mind had been unable to settle. I didn't allow myself to think about sitting on the table with Chase; instead, I chose to fixate on our poker game. Something had been bothering me about the game. The win had been too easy. Card games are half luck, but Chase had been acting strangely before my win. Pandering with questions and distractions before he showed his cards. I almost didn't want to say it, or think it, but...had he somehow thrown the game? Lost on purpose?

The thought humiliated me. Especially since I had done, not one, but two victory dance laps around the table after my win. A small part of me, probably the warm and comfortably dressed in his sweats and sweatshirt part, felt touched by the gesture. Either way, I had to figure this out, because I couldn't gloat or tease him anymore if my win wasn't a true win. But, he would never let me win. Would he? Of course, the whole thing was his idea, with the thought to get me some clothes. So maybe he was trying to ease his conscience. Still, Chase Riley letting me win? I wouldn't stand for it.

How did he do it? What was so off about the game?

After thinking about it a bit longer, to no avail, I peeled off the covers and got out of bed. I re-rolled the bottoms of Chase's sweats up to keep them from dragging on the floor and rolled the elastic waistband a couple of times to make the cinch tighter around my waist. The sweatshirt was also too big, but other than pulling up the sleeves, I couldn't do much to help it. I wouldn't win any fashion contests, especially with the boxer briefs I was wearing, but I had never felt better.

That being said, I only ventured out to the kitchen after I had showered, put on my makeup, brushed my teeth, and if I'm being completely honest—shaved my legs.

Chase stood in the living room, putting on a pair of fishing waders over his coveralls. He looked up and scanned my clothing with his eyes. Okay, I guess the only thing visible was his clothing. Though he didn't look my way for long, I didn't detect any lingering effect of yesterday in his eyes.

"Looking good, Blister. I like your style," Chase said. Good, we were back to Blister again. I found it was much easier to keep him and thoughts of him at bay when 'Blister' was between us.

"Ha," I said, making my way to the kitchen, hitching up the sweatpants as I walked. As comfortable as they were, keeping them upright on my body all week might prove challenging.

"What are you doing?" I asked over my shoulder, while I filled a glass with water.

When he didn't answer right away, I turned back to look at him.

He held his hands outstretched and gestured to his clothing as if I had missed something very obvious. "I'll give you one wild guess."

"Off to a wedding?"

He snorted and pulled a beanie on his head. "Wanna come?"

"Thanks, but it would probably start to get embarrassing for you when I out fish you again."

He stamped his feet in his boots, gathering up his tackle box and fishing gear, before adding, "Awww, but I'd sure have fun watching you try."

"Sorry, I've got to get some writing done today." I opened the fridge for a snack out of habit, only to be disappointed. I eyed the pack of eggs, my mouth watering. A quick peek inside and I saw he only had about six eggs left from the pack of 18. I couldn't do it. I sighed and grabbed another pack of maple sugar oatmeal from the cupboard. I refused to check the expiration date on the box, but the pack was hard and stuck together like glue. Only after adding water and some coaxing with a fork did it finally mix together and resemble coarse oatmeal. Just a quick buzz in the microwave and it would soon resemble thick, tan sludge.

Bon Appétit.

"If I'm not back in two hours, send a search party," Chase quipped as he opened the door, somewhat awkwardly, gear in hand.

I sent him off with a wave. "Bring me home a hamburger."

He stuck his head back inside the door. "Still no mustard?"

I met his amused gaze in surprise. My heart lurched—my body warmed. How could he have remembered that tiny detail about me? There were many Friday nights where Matt and our group would grab hamburgers, but I hadn't realized my mustard aversion would be something someone would remember.

Then he winked and said, "Bye, Penny."

The door closed before I could say anything else, leaving me feeling funny, flattered, warm, like I didn't want him to leave, and just a tiny bit confused by that wink.

7

B last it.

    That dang wink completely ruined the productive afternoon I had planned. Instead of typing furiously for my book, I found myself re-playing the wink and the mustard comment a thousand times. Each time the daydreams got a bit more farfetched. The last ended with a kiss, and that's when I jumped up from the couch to do a few laps around the cramped cabin and grab a glass of water. Mercy. It couldn't have been that long since a man had shown me attention. It was literally the tiniest amount of attention ever, and I was playing it in my mind like I had just been given the crown jewels.

    I brought my thoughts around to my last boyfriend, Conner. It had ended about three months ago—mostly on the basis of my roommate Connie, who told us we had the chemistry and excitement of a rock. Conner, who was a Geology professor at our local community college, had been flattered. I broke up with him the very next day. Honestly, other than my grocery budget lasting longer, and the fact that my evenings were spent watching TV by myself, I hadn't noticed much difference in my life without him.

    It occurred to me that none of the breakups in my life had been devastating. At least not for me. Certainly, no man I went out with had ever thought to wink at me. I didn't even know winking was still a thing. Was it?

Had every guy I dated been so vanilla? This idea was hitting me hard enough that I had to sit down. Conner, Trevor, Greg... All of them were nice, quiet, smart, safe—boring. Mostly great qualities, probably why I was drawn to them. All of them were very active in their careers—each in some sort of scientific type profession that I could never speak to them about because I understood nothing they would tell me. We would have nice evenings out every once in a while, chuckle over our days together, and probably would have led a pleasant existence if something had ever worked out.

But what I couldn't understand was why I had dated virtually the same type of man since high school. I had always been confused and would roll my eyes at the overly dramatic way roommates and friends would break up, or get broken up with. So much angst, crying, and emotional drama. I had no experience with that. Every breakup of mine seemed more like parting ways from a business deal than having any sort of emotional effect.

Had I been attracted to any of them? Yes. No? Maybe? They were each handsome enough in their own right. I was never embarrassed to be seen with them. Each of them adequate, if a bit reserved in the social department, but I never felt their presence in a room. I knew they were there, but I never *felt* them there.

The last few days living with Chase had been supercharged with *him*. I knew where he was at all times. Not in a creepy way, but in a way that kept me on edge. I was both nervous and excited to see Chase whenever he appeared, even though I played it cool. When we sat near each other on the couch, I was aware of every movement. Anytime our skin made contact, the touch had charged through my body.

Was that what being attracted to someone felt like?

Goodness, it was exhausting to not be able to concentrate all day long. Even when he wasn't there, I was still obsessing over the tiniest bit of nothing. Granted, it was hard not to *feel* him there. One of his long-sleeved shirts lay flung over the couch. The fishing gear he hadn't needed sat haphazardly on the table and partially on one of the kitchen chairs.

Throughout all my productive writing time, I had imagined Hallmark movie scenarios in my head, where we'd be doing dishes together, our fingertips brushing in the water. Or playing another round of poker, only *not* the version where we were putting *on* clothes. Alright, I'm kidding. I only got as far as him taking off his *shirt*. I forced my daydreams to stop there, but I couldn't help taking one tiny second more to dwell on those abs. Or even him just looking over at me with his teasing eyes and a smart-alec grin. That one stopped me in my tracks. The teasing eyes were my favorite part of Chase, I realized. None of my boyfriends had teasing eyes. Kind eyes, which were also important, but not teasing.

I hated the teasing. Didn't I? I sure thought I did in high school but, deep down, wasn't Chase the reason I re-adjusted my makeup before every Friday night hang out? The few nights he wasn't there, I usually went to bed early.

The clock on the wall read 4 pm. No wonder I was feeling hungry. Restless. I reached into the fridge, about to steal just one egg, when I whirled around and looked again at the clock. 4 pm. Chase had left at noon. He mentioned he'd be back in two hours. He was two hours late. How could I have missed that? I raced to the small kitchen window, looking out toward the lake, hidden by a cluster of trees next to the cabin. The sun had already set past the mountains, and darkness would soon be settling in. Only one set of tracks were visible, leading toward the lake.

I looked again at the clock, willing it to turn itself back to the appropriate time. Should I go look for him? What if something happened? What if he slipped through the ice? My heart was pounding as I rushed over to the coat rack and flung my arms through the sleeves. I was just reaching for my boots when I stopped. What if Chase was completely fine? He probably just lost track of time. The man came out all this way to fish, he obviously knew what he was doing. If I came rushing out there to find him, I would *never* hear the end of it. The thought of his teasing alone was enough to redden my cheeks and caused me to shrug out of my coat. He was probably fine. I would give it another few minutes and then re-evaluate.

I marched back to the couch and sat down. My feet tapped against the floor. The tick of the clock sounded through the cabin like a drum. My fingers itched for something to do. I glanced around and picked up the Louis L'Amour book Chase had been reading the day before. Great. I would read a book, relax for a bit while I waited for Chase to come back. Not that I was waiting for him, I was just...taking a break. He was only a couple of hours late. Not a big deal on the mountain. Time didn't matter much up here. I opened the book to the first page and did my finest attempt at reading. It would be dark soon, so he would definitely be heading back any minute. I didn't need to worry. I re-read the first line of the book.

It would be dark soon.

Which meant if Chase was in trouble I had only a small window of daylight left to find him. I turned around to stare at the back door, begging it to open. When it didn't, I stood up. My heart began to pound so loud I could hear it in my eardrum. Teasing or no, there was no kidding myself any longer. I had to find Chase. I stuffed my feet in my snow boots and grabbed a beanie, slipping it over my hair before yanking open the door and stepping outside.

The snow came down in big flakes as I attempted to step into Chase's partially covered boot tracks in the snow. My eyes scanned through the trees for any sign of him. I made my feet walk when I wanted to run. I couldn't afford to slip and break an ankle. When I made it past the trees and into the clearing before the lake, I called out Chase's name. When I didn't hear anything, I looked down and found his tracks on the south side and followed them around the base of the lake, calling his name as I went.

Inwardly, I was panicking, but I was trying to talk my mind out of a full hysteria. He just lost track of time. He was probably just kidding about the two-hour thing. I'm sure he was used to staying out all day, and I was going to look like a crazy person when I found him.

My foot caught on a root sprawled across the length of the pathway, hidden by the fresh snow, and I went sprawling, landing on my hands and knees with a hard thud. I hadn't taken the time to find gloves before leaving the cabin, and now my hands were red with scratches from my fall. I stood on shaky legs, brushing off the snow, my eyes constantly in motion when I saw something. Through the trees, Chase stood, minding a pole about two hundred yards away. Relief flooded out of my body in the form of a sigh. Once my breath was spent, anger and annoyance quickly replaced it. Why wasn't he responding? Didn't he hear me calling?

From where I stood, the trail seemed to diverge, with a small split leading toward Chase onto the ice. Although it was difficult to tell with the snow piling up so quickly, there were definite footprints along the new path. They had to be Chase's. Calling to him again with still no answer, I gritted my teeth and began to make my way toward him. Stepping out of the clearing, I took a few hesitant steps onto the ice and snow-covered lake. Chase's back was still turned away from me. Slowly, I made my way toward him, testing each step before adding my full weight. Halfway toward Chase, I stopped when the ice below my feet began popping. I held myself still, afraid to take another step.

I yelled his name once more. This time, Chase turned toward me, startling when he saw me. He yanked out his earbuds, dropping them to the ground.

"Blister, what are you doing out here?"

My body stood, paralyzed from fear. I began speaking too loud and too fast, all at once. "It's after four. You left at noon. You told me to come find you after two hours. The ice is popping right here—should it be doing that?"

His face tightened as he surveyed the area at my feet. "Stay right there. Don't move."

He grabbed his pole and in one smooth move, he had cut the line set up in the small hole. He began inching his way toward me. As he got closer, the ground beneath me began to shift, ever so slightly, gurgling and yielding.

"Stop. It's getting louder. Don't come any closer."

He stopped, his hand held out, palms up as if trying to soothe a frightened animal. "Okay. Why don't you try backing up the way you came?"

My heartbeat was in my throat at this point. My body felt paralyzed. I was afraid to move or breathe, the ground beneath me felt so unstable. "Chase...I don't think I can move."

Chase swore, looking around at our surroundings desperately, fear now etched on his face as well. "Okay, the only option right now is for you to back up slowly. I'll try to back up and come toward you at a different angle."

"No, please don't go." The fear had taken over all of my senses. I wanted Chase where I could see him.

"Penny, you can do this."

I took a deep breath and looked down at my feet. The ground seemed to move at each twist of my head or slight shift in my stance. "I don't think this spot can handle my full weight. If I lift the other leg to go backward, the ice will break." The words sputtered out in a whisper, but he seemed to understand.

Chase stared at my feet, and then the snow-crusted lake we stood on, before nodding. "Okay, you're right. I'm going to back up slowly here and make my way toward the shoreline, and then I'll come at you from the side. The trees keep it covered from the sun, so it should be strong enough. Wait until I'm set up before you move, so I can be in a good position to help you if I need to."

Too scared to nod my head, I whispered, "Okay."

It felt like a lifetime before Chase had made his way over toward me. He stopped about five yards away. He was coming at me from the side now, but I couldn't turn my head. Relief poured through my veins as he neared, even while my body trembled against my will. He stepped another yard closer. The ground beneath me popped as he did so. He stopped when he heard it too. My pounding heart reverberated throughout my entire body, touching every nerve until I shook with fear.

"Alright, I want you to reach out slowly and grab the end of my fishing pole. And then don't let go."

"I don't think I can turn to look at you."

"Just hold out your arm and I'll place the pole in your hand."

My breathing became deep and guttural as I slowly lifted my shaking arm. The popping and cracking on the ice sounded in my ears. The small shift of my weight as I lifted my arm to the side, toward Chase, proved to be my downfall. A loud crack rang out and just as I felt the tip of Chase's pole touch my open palm, the frozen floor beneath me fell, dropping me with a startled scream into the dark, glacial abyss.

It was several long moments before I felt the cold. At first, it was only the pain of a thousand sharp needles, jabbing into my skin on contact. The heart-stopping, bone-chilling panic didn't start for a few seconds into my drop. Once I started to rise to the top for air, my head hit something, stopping my ascent. The ice. Panicked, I began flailing my arms, with as much energy as my shocked body could muster. I forced my eyes to open and I quickly located the light—the small hole I fell from. My breath was running out and my head kept hitting the top of the ice. I inched my way toward the light, nearly there, when two arms lunged into the water, locking under my armpits, and pulled me up, over and out of the water in an instant.

I fell backward on top of him, both of us releasing a groan. For a moment, we laid there, the shock of what just happened hanging heavy over us, before my body began shaking violently.

"Come on, Penny," Chase mumbled, as he climbed out from underneath me. "This ice won't hold us."

With some effort on his part, he scooted us both toward the shore. When the sounds of the popping ice stilled, he removed his heavy coat and threw it over my shoulders.

"We have to get to the house now!" His voice was loud in my ear. I wanted to tell him to stop shouting at me. Everything was okay, but I couldn't recall if the words ever left my throat. My steps slowed. My brain felt foggy. I was just so cold. Chase had a tight grip around my shoulders, leading me off the ice, but at some point, I could no longer feel my legs moving. Then, I was floating. The blur of the trees passed all around me. Large snowflakes landed on my nose. The world seemed very quiet all of a sudden. Peaceful even.

More shouting in my ear. Chase. I couldn't figure out what he was trying to tell me. More sounds. The stomping of feet on the hard ground, the swishing sound his coat made against the friction of our bodies. Was he running? The creak of the door. The familiar smell of pine and moths when we entered the cabin.

Home.

I didn't pass out. I didn't faint. Yet, I wasn't alert in any real sense, I was just—numb. Frozen. My world was the blur before the glasses came on. The sounds around me were muffled, as though I were listening from underwater. I felt skin against mine and I hissed, trying to move away. Away from the fire. The heat. More shouting, and then, I felt someone pulling me closer. It had to be Chase. Was he shivering?

Sharp needles seemed to rub up and down my arms and legs, pricking and biting at my senses. I thrashed about, trying to move away from the hurt, but I couldn't move. My limbs wouldn't cooperate and the weight upon me didn't give an inch.

Sometime later, the sound of a crackling fire drew me to awareness once more. The sharp jabs in my arms and legs had begun to subside, and I could see Chase rubbing my body with his hands. What time was it? The darkness of the night had seeped into the cabin. The warm, orange glow from the roaring fire our only light. I closed my eyes once more, and this time, I slept.

When I awoke in the dark sometime later, I felt another sensation. Warmth. Though I couldn't piece together the reasons why, my cheek was pressed against something heated. A body. A chest, maybe. Chase's chest. My hand was somewhere warm. Was that Chase's armpit? My mind felt as if it were trying to wade through a thick soup. I couldn't conjure up the energy to process anything, so once more, I closed my eyes.

8

The cozy heat that had blanketed me the past few hours stood—abandoning our cocoon of warmth. At the shift in body temperature, my eyes flicked open and watched as Chase added more logs to the fire, wearing only a pair of basketball shorts. When he turned back toward me, I met his gaze. He disappeared behind me into the kitchen for some time. When he returned, he knelt down beside me.

"You need to drink something warm. It's just hot chocolate."

I complied, and he helped me sit up enough to lean against the couch. When the blanket across my shoulders fell to my waist, I felt him fix the blanket once more. He held the cup against my mouth to help me drink before I took the cup from his hand. He acquiesced but sat next to me on our pile of makeshift blankets strewn all over the floor.

I took a few sips before setting the cup down on the coffee table, my blanket falling down again while I did so. This time, I squeaked out a protest in shock as I took in, for the first time, how I was dressed. Okay, I had seen all those movies, even written a few short stories, and everybody knows that when you fall into a frozen lake and somebody has to rescue you, the clothes come off. But I'm here to tell you, nobody is prepared for the shock of waking up in only your bra and underwear, knowing full well that the hot guy was the one to take them off. I just thanked my lucky stars that I had brought a razor on this trip, and the fact that having a surprise man in the house meant I had used it recently.

"Don't worry, I was too worried about you dying from hypothermia to appreciate what I was doing," Chase said, wryly. He stood quickly and walked toward the hallway. "I'll go grab you some clothes."

He returned a moment later and tossed me a pair of his shorts and his long-sleeved t-shirt. Lying to the side of our makeshift bed were the wet clothes we had been wearing when I fell in the lake. He gathered up the pile and headed toward the laundry room. He kicked the door closed, giving me just enough time to convince my stiff limbs to cooperate and dress myself. I knew it was silly to crave modesty when he was literally the one who took *off* my clothes, but I hurried anyway.

A few moments later, he took a tentative step out into the hallway, the sound of the washer humming behind him. "You good?"

"Yeah."

I shivered slightly as I pulled the blankets back up to my shoulders, watching as he entered the living room. "I like a man who knows his way around a washing machine."

His soft eyes met mine as he approached me once again. "Good to know."

He settled back down on the pillows beside me, maneuvering me in one swift, hot movement so I was lying across his chest. Instant warmth seeped back into my chest and body, and I found I had no strength to resist him, even as he sucked in a breath.

"Dang girl, you still feel like ice. What happened to the fishing pole idea? Why didn't you hold on?"

"I'm going to be honest; I didn't think about that stupid pole for one second after I dropped through the ice."

He chuckled lightly as he ran his hands briskly across my back. "Fair enough."

"Why the fire?"

"Power was out when I brought you in last night. It seems to be working now."

"Sounds about right."

"Yup."

"I could really go for a hot bath right about now."

"I'd love to help get you into one."

I held back a smile as elation surged through my senses. "Just know, if I had the strength to lift my arm, I would smack you for that."

I sensed his smile. "That comment was almost as good."

"Chase?"

"Yeah?"

"Thanks."

"Anytime, Blister." A slight pause and then he added, "Penny."

His arms pulled me tighter against him. Was that a reflex? Or did he mean to do that? We laid in contemplative silence for a few minutes before Chase added, "Will this cancel out whatever made you hate me back in the day?"

"What?"

"What made you hate me when we were kids?"

"I never hated you."

He shifted and lifted his head up, looming above me, a challenging glint in his eyes. "Come on, Penny. Let's have it out. You couldn't stand me. And it made no sense because I'm a delight."

I couldn't tell him. I wouldn't. How immature would it be to actually say the words? Those stupid, childish words that have haunted my existence since the day they were uttered, so much middle school bravado behind them. They shouldn't have meant as much as they did, but here we were. And then, they came out.

"'She looks like my dog, but not as hot.'"

He squinted down at me in confusion. "Huh?"

I chuckled dryly, an attempt to appear indifferent after all these years, but my heart pounded at the confession. "I overheard you say that to some of your friends in eighth grade. You were talking about me."

"I never said that." Chase looked horrified at the thought. His hand on my shoulder stopped rubbing. "Why would I say that?"

I pasted a light smile on my face, as though this conversation amused me. Even though the tension in the room had heightened. "It's fine. It's not a big deal anymore, but at the time... I think that's why."

He still looked confused, as if he were trying to piece together a time and place. I helped him. "You said it to Pete Davis by your locker in 8th grade."

"Pete Davis?"

"Yeah, he moved away that next year, I think."

Awareness dimmed in his eyes, along with something else. Embarrassment? Shame? I found I couldn't stand looking at it, so I added quickly, "It's not a big deal, I promise. But you asked. That was probably why I had a hard time being nice to you."

He was silent for a long time. I imagined myself digging a hole in the ground, and never coming out. Why had I told him? Nothing could make it any better. He would just feel awkward now, and I would feel petty.

"I'm sorry."

Whatever I thought he would say, a simple apology was definitely not it. And somehow, it made the whole exchange even worse.

Turning back to face him I said, "Look, I shouldn't have told you. I think all the smoke and cold is getting to me. It's not a big deal, I get it. It was middle school. Everybody says stupid things. It's not like I've thought about it every day since. I just overheard it, and then decided to find stupid ways to retaliate, I guess."

He laid on his back, still looking contemplative. "You know, there was a time when I had just joined the football team and had been trying to get in Pete's good graces. He was the captain. I would have probably said anything to try to make him think I was cool. But after I realized what a jerk he was, I left it alone. And then he moved."

"I'm pretty sure he was the one responsible for spray painting the teacher's lounge," I added.

"Sounds about right."

We laid in silence. My heartbeat drummed a million miles an hour in my ear. Why did I say that? Why did I mention it? It only succeeded in making me feel small and childish.

"Do you want to know what I wanted to do the other night when I saw you in your underwear?"

My eyes widened. "Chase, I promise, you don't have to…"

"I wanted to kiss you. You walked past me, and it was all I could do not to… And then you started wearing *my* underwear and it was even worse."

My mouth dropped open as I stared at him, stunned.

He held up his hands in peace. "I never *saw* you wearing mine, I didn't have to. I have a great imagination. So, tell that to your four-teen-year-old self. You're hot."

Fighting the heat rising my cheeks, I said, "Stop. You don't have to do this. I promise I'm fine. Completely over it. I shouldn't have said anything. I'm the only female trapped in this cabin with you—if it were my grandma here instead of me, you'd probably be saying the same things to her."

I laughed into his chest at the horrified face he pulled, but I had meant every word. I knew all this sounded like I was an insecure, little girl seeking reassurance from the man who did her wrong all those years ago.

And that's exactly what it was.

I was that girl, and I needed reassurance. It was that simple. I had been fine without it because I never thought I'd see Chase again after high school. Never contemplated a relationship with him. Now, things were different. Now, I needed it.

"I had a crush on you in high school."

My head shot up to meet his eyes. "No you didn't."

"I did. Ask Matt."

"What? No way. He would have told me."

"I believe his exact words were, 'You touch her, and I'll kill you. And if she ever finds out, she'll probably kill you, too.'"

I drew in my breath. I could hear Matt saying the words perfectly. The perks of having an overprotective twin brother.

"From his glowing recommendation, I gathered the feelings wouldn't be reciprocated, so I just kept annoying you for attention. And you kept hating me, so we all won, I guess."

"I didn't know."

"Would it have changed anything if you had?"

The cold and the heat underneath our blankets were beginning to be a doozy. It felt intimate to have a heart-to-heart conversation when you are literally heart-to-heart. I couldn't look at him any longer. I laid my head on his chest while he cleared his throat and rubbed his hand briskly over my arm to warm it.

It was already warm.

"I'm not sure," I said into his chest. And I wasn't sure. If I had known he liked me in high school, would that have changed me? Softened me toward him?

My feet and legs were still freezing, so I wheedled my way in between his legs, smiling slightly as he hissed when my cold feet touched his. Things were getting confusing. I needed to move, to break our contact and get up from his cozy body of warmth. I just couldn't bring myself to care. I would care tomorrow when my brain wasn't so foggy, and my eyes weren't so heavy. When Chase's arms weren't locked around me so tight.

"Chase?" I asked, drowsy again and perhaps a bit lightheaded. Somehow, in my half-unconscious state, I had finally solved a puzzle that had been plaguing me since the day before.

"Yeah?" He mumbled as if he were almost asleep.

"You lost with the Jack of Hearts yesterday."

"Huh?"

"The Jack of Hearts was my throwaway card. You switched it out of the discard pile with one of your cards and let me win, didn't you?"

There was a long pause, but then, in a faraway voice, he said, "Sure doesn't sound like something I'd do, Blister."

I said no more, but my heart leaped into my throat as he pulled me closer, tucking me in with his arms and warming my body. Even the term Blister had somehow lost its sting. Tonight, falling from his lips, it almost sounded...endearing, sweet. To any onlooker from the window, this would have seemed like a scene for lovers. As I felt myself drift off to sleep, feeling the way his fingers rhythmically rubbed my arm, it was beginning to seem that way to me too.

It was still dark outside. I figured it was probably five or six in the morning, but there was no way to know because there was no way I was moving a muscle to do anything dumb, like check my phone, or the clock, or to pee. If I moved, then this would all go away, and I quite enjoyed the sound of Chase's deep and steady breathing in my ear. He even mumbled in his sleep once, and it was the most adorable thing.

Oh geez, the next few days needed to go fast. I had to get out of there. The cabin was feeling much too cozy. Even my thoughts toward Chase had been much more generous and forgiving than they had ever been before.

Look, here's the thing—there's nothing to forgive between Chase and me. It was all a long time ago. I've moved on. I've dated plenty. I've gained confidence in my talents and abilities, and even (for the most part) my looks. At least before I found myself stuck in a cabin with Chase Riley.

Even though I know we were both in junior high, and the comment was probably meaningless, I'd be lying to myself if I said I hadn't thought about it since.

She looks like my dog, but not as hot.

So childish. So middle school. So dumb.

So not something you ever forget.

That's the thing about middle school. It stays with you. Sometimes, it's stuck in that unconscious part of your brain. Sometimes, you don't hear from it for a while. Sometimes, you thought you'd forgotten, but during a moment of doubt, it was the first comment in my head.

That moment changed me.

Instead of striving for beauty like the rest of my friends, that was the day I decided to become funny. Witty. Snarky. If I couldn't be beautiful, being funny was the next best thing. I had dedicated my entire life to being self-deprecating and sarcastic. To let others know that I knew I wasn't pretty, but that it was okay because I was the one who made them laugh. Soon after, junior high faded into high school. I saw less and less of Chase, as he became immersed in the sports scene.

Then, something unexpected happened. Matt joined the golf team. He and Chase were put together as partners and hit it off. Middle school had been tough, but through it all, I had Matt. My twin. He was always there, and when he was there, that meant we were together. A team. But then suddenly, he had friends I didn't have, joined a sport I wasn't involved in, and went to parties I was never invited to. At first, he would ask if I wanted to go, but I knew *who* else would be in the car and I declined every time. After a while, he stopped asking. I took a quieter, more behind-the-scenes route at the school newspaper. There, my snark and wittiness paid off, and soon I was writing a weekly column detailing the daily life of a student.

In our junior year, Matt joined the football team as well, thanks to Chase's influence. Then, I couldn't avoid Chase because he was always in my home. If sports jokes and niceness were Matt's thing, snark and wit became mine. Chase gave as much as he took, which led to some interesting movie nights in our living room. At that point, I had discovered that if I wanted to keep my brother and me close, I would have to endure a few football parties at my house every week. And to be honest, I found myself having a nice time, more often than not. Not that I would have admitted that to anyone.

The newspaper column got me a full-ride scholarship to college and became a great platform for my life as a writer. So, there was a lot of good in my life that stemmed from that one little comment.

But all of a sudden, here I was, once again, awkward and unsure. A couple of nights locked in a cabin with Chase and I discovered that the small crack of insecurity in my foundation never really went away. It got covered up and forgotten, but at the cabin, I had to face it. I had to face *him*.

Now, I'm left wondering who has cracks in their foundation from a thoughtless comment made by me?

My pride had been stung by this boy a long time ago. I bit back with humor and verbal jabs, which had always suited our tepid relationship just fine. It was all a game to him, and while he knew nothing of the real reason behind it, it hid something much deeper for me.

But that morning, I found myself awake, and for the first time since I arrived at the cabin, my body wasn't shaking with cold. My skin felt smooth in the absence of goosebumps. My head lay nestled in that perfect spot on a man's arm. His hand covered mine as it lay pressed against his chest. The soft rhythm of his breathing lifted our hands up and down, while one of my legs was thrown carelessly around his. All of this was wrapped neatly inside a large, flannel blanket.

At great risk to his own well-being, he had saved my life.

Chase Riley had saved my life. Now I lay next to this man, who once called me a dog, while he held me in his arms as if I were something precious.

And it's making me second guess everything.

9

We awoke on Thursday morning, coiled together like sleepy snakes. The fire had died sometime in the early morning. When I breathed, puffs of chilled, white air escaped my mouth. I lay with my head perched on Chase's chest and my body nestled into his. I wasn't sure if I was too embarrassed to make eye contact, or if I was too reluctant to move away from his heated body. Chase took a deep breath as he released my hand on his chest to rub his eyes for a moment.

My breath caught as the fingers on his hand that was curled against me, stroked my arm softly for just a second. Did he realize?

"You sure go through a lot of work just to sleep with me."

I hit him on the chest as he laughed. Chase gently disentangled our limbs and pulled back the cover of our blanket, as he jumped up to add more logs to the fire, a rush of frigid air taking his place.

Two days until Christmas. Two days until Chase had to leave the cabin. I would stay, awaiting Matt and Gina's arrival. It all seemed too fast. We had just gotten on friendly terms and soon he had to leave.

Chase touched the light switch and looked over at me and said, "Fingers crossed." He flipped the switch and to our surprise, the bulb flickered on, brightening the room with a hazy, yellow hue.

"Guess we aren't going to starve today," Chase said, as he wandered toward the hallway. "And I'm turning on the heat in all the rooms."

I stretched my sore limbs before standing up. I don't know why my body still felt so tired. My eyes squinted at the clock in the kitchen. Eight in the morning. I had slept for nearly fourteen hours. Did nearly drowning and being saved by a hot guy from hypothermia cause fatigue? I heard Chase step into the bathroom and turn the shower on while I started folding up the blankets that were strewn all over the floor. Either way, a little physical distance between Chase and me was probably a good thing at this point. I had basically used him as a human pillow all night and enjoyed every minute of it.

I switched the laundry and flitted about the cabin, tidying up. Or told myself that's what I was doing. I just wanted to be busy, or at least look busy so that when Chase emerged and I had to face him again, he might not be able to tell how much the night before had affected me.

I did inventory on our supplies. We had two large potatoes, one package of bacon, four eggs, a few granola bars, some oatmeal packets, hot chocolate, and half a refrigerator filled with fresh-caught fish. When a fully dressed and delicious smelling Chase walked into the kitchen, I was proud to have something useful to report to him. Maybe if I talked about fish all the time, it would keep my mind from wandering back to his warm chest and light touch.

We were both sick of fish. Well, I was always sick of fish, but this time, even Chase admitted he wasn't feeling it that day. Since neither of us wanted to expose ourselves to the memories of the place that nearly killed us the day before, we seemed to form some sort of silent agreement that neither of us would be venturing outside for our food.

"Would you like to share some of my bacon?" I asked, lightening the mood. The gleaming, annoyed look he shot me made the whole comment worth it.

That was the beginning of our new dance.

Two steps forward, one step back. Cha-cha-cha. The back and forth between the awkward and the familiar. Snark and sweet. Bold and timid. We had tread upon new ground the night before, and neither of us had found our steady footing. New territory was yet to be discovered. We now knew it was there, within reach, we just hadn't found it yet.

In the middle of mundane tasks, like washing dishes or tidying up —our gazes would meet with sheepish smiles. Over and over it happened, until I was a bundle of nerves, and very much aware of how awkward my hands were. Even walking became difficult when I felt his eyes on me. At the table, eating our bowls of petrified oatmeal and two slices of bacon, his legs had brushed against mine...twice.

What was happening? It was *Chase Riley*, for heaven's sake.

All to myself.

Chase, for his part, remained a charming tease but kept his distance. Well, as much distance as a nine hundred square foot cabin could afford.

Probably for the best.

It turned out the power was dancing too. It went back off after breakfast and flickered on and off throughout the rest of the day. We had granola bars and milk for lunch. Around dinner time, our growling stomachs kept us near the kitchen to be ready to fry up some fish if we had the chance. It didn't necessarily sound good to me, but it was a hot meal, and warmth was something I craved.

We had spent a quiet day together. Chase lounged on the couch, reading a book he'd found at the cabin, while I spent time curled up in the easy chair, writing. I hadn't planned on staying there all day, I usually did my best writing in my room, alone. But the warmth of the fire drew me like a bear to honey. I had Chase's freshly washed sweatpants with my tank top, paired with his large sweatshirt. I also wore a pair of his socks, and I had never been cozier.

The words poured out of me.

Near 6 pm, the lights flickered on and off for almost a minute before finally staying on. We waited a few moments, staring at the lights, making certain. After a minute of no flickers, we raced into the kitchen. Chase grabbed the frying pan and began heating it up, while I rummaged through the stinky piles of dead fish carcasses for our dinner. I grabbed the two smallest ones I could find.

"I'm glad to see your taste in food is improving," Chase said. He reached out to grab the fish wrapped in foil that I held out to him, our fingers brushing on contact.

"Desperate times," I replied, bumping him with my hip as I stood next to him at the stove. He placed the fish on the hot pan, where it popped and sizzled against the heat.

"That smells like death."

Chase grinned as he put his arm around my shoulders, drawing me in close. "I love your sweet talk."

We fried the fish up in the small kitchen, amid accidental brushing, nudging, and teasing. I believe there was even a wink thrown around in the ring. All through dinner, my heart was in a constant state of flutter. Anticipation swelled in my breast at every touch. At the table, we sat corner to corner, our legs brushing and even kicking at times, as we laughed, ate our fish, and drank our hot chocolate. My nerves made the food wonderfully tasteless in my mouth. My heart was flying first into battle, while my head was trying to reason with it, attempting more caution.

I felt Chase's eyes on me. I looked up and met his gaze, pushing a strand of my hair back behind my ear as I did so.

"Popcorn and a movie?" he asked.

I smiled. "Yeah."

Caution, caution, caution, my head warned. My stubborn heart willfully ignored the plea.

Soon, the fishy smell of the cabin was overpowered by popcorn and butter. For all the cabin didn't have, we were elated to find an air popper and a bag of kernels in the laundry room, earlier that day. I thanked the heavens that we had found a stray stick of butter in the back of the fridge. I wasn't going to think about how long it could have been there. Beggars couldn't be choosers, and I was feeling quite grateful that night. As we rummaged through the eclectic shelves stuffed full of video cassette tapes, the air between us was pinging.

Electric.

Both of us were feeling in the Christmas mood and we settled on 'It's a Wonderful Life.' Chase plopped down on the left side of the couch, while I rewound the tape in the tape rewinder before pushing it inside the VCR.

"Good thing my grandma had a VHS player at her house growing up, or we might never have figured this out," I said.

"I knew being in a cabin with a grandma in training would come in handy this week."

A comment like that, I could not abide. Grabbing the popcorn bowl off the table, I stepped over his feet that were propped up on the coffee table, ignored his motioning for me to sit by him, and sat on the complete opposite end of the couch.

"What the?"

I looked over at him and met his playful affront with my stare.

"You take all my clothes and then you sit clear over there? With the popcorn bowl?"

"I've seen you eat popcorn, I think I should get a few minutes head start."

Chase smiled, shook his head, and turned toward the TV when the movie began to start.

A few minutes later, I looked over to Chase, shivering on his side of the couch. Dramatically, I might add.

"What's wrong?" I asked him, feeling a bit suspicious.

He looked over at me, a teasing gleam in his eye. "I'm freezing. How are you?"

I dropped my blanket and got up off the couch, sauntering toward him. He stopped shivering immediately, anticipation warming his eyes as he watched me approach. And then...I kept walking to the other side of the TV and grabbed the brown ratty cabin blanket. I hit him with it as I walked by him, once again settling down on my side of the couch, amid his deep chuckle.

Throughout the first half of the movie, I was aware of movement to the left of me. Chase was constantly getting up to grab a drink, use the bathroom, or refill his popcorn bowl. It wasn't until George Bailey had married his Mary, that I realized he was now only an arm's length away from me.

I eyed him suspiciously out of the corner of my eye. He seemed intent on the movie, mindlessly eating popcorn, same as me. Confused, I turned my attention back to the movie. Had he been clear on the other side of the couch? Maybe he hadn't been as far as I thought?

Chase stood up again, walking to the kitchen and filling his cup by the sink. When he turned back around, his eyes scanned the room and landed on mine before I jolted and focused my attention back on the TV.

Except, now there was no way I could focus on what was in front of me when to the side of me all I could see was the blur of Chase walking closer. Seriously, was he walking in slow motion? My heart had pulses all over my body. I slunk down ever so slightly into the couch, pulling the blanket up higher as he settled back down on the couch next to me. His arm and leg brushed against mine, sending fire racing from my head to my fingertips.

My gaze was fixed on the movie, even when I felt him turn and look at me. I couldn't look. I couldn't acknowledge it. Him. He stared blatantly, for so long that my mouth betrayed me, and even my attempt to bite my lip couldn't keep the smile from forming; along with two heated spots of color in my cheeks, and my rapidly beating heart.

I felt his smile before he turned his attention back to the TV.

A few moments later, my blanket was being tugged across my lap.

Glancing over, he gave me a charming grin. "I'm cold."

All thoughts fled as he entered my space. I was helpless to stop him. My heartbeat trumpeted in my ears. The movie forgotten. Had there ever been any other thoughts in my head before now? This was

Chase Riley. How could I let this happen? It wasn't supposed to be Chase, but I only had thoughts of him. He had moved past my defensive barrier, and before I realized what had happened, the enemy had invaded. The blanket was protecting my space. Protecting *me*. Protecting my hands from being held, my body from being touched, and my heart from being broken. Attraction was one thing—a relationship was another. I had just let him in, and my stupid body was reacting to him—just like I was afraid of.

I shifted toward him when I should have moved away. When our hands brushed across each other under the blanket, I didn't pull back. When his fingers reached out to grab my hand, I let him.

For a long while, he held my hand under the warm blanket. He stroked my palm and played with the rings on my fingers—and it felt amazing. For my part, the fuss and resistance I had initially felt to offer, dissipated like the smoke in the warm fire blazing before us. My head found its way to his shoulder and after a moment, he released my hand and put his arm around me. I curled into his warm body, my head on his chest, and my fingers splayed across his shirt.

The plight of George Bailey was long forgotten as I closed my eyes and relished the embrace.

I awoke sometime in the night. My neck felt stiff as I tried to get my bearings. This was the third time in two days I had fallen asleep on Chase. Either he was extremely boring or extremely comfortable. Unfortunately, my heart knew exactly which answer it was. The fire had cooled to embers, the glow of the TV the only light in the room. Underneath my head, Chase's chest rose and fell in a deep rhythm, clearly asleep. There was something so cozy—so lovely about falling asleep with someone. As much as I wanted to stay in this embrace and fall back asleep, the two cups of hot chocolate had taken their toll.

As gently as I could manage, I uncurled myself from his arms and removed my hand from his grasp on his chest. I left his side and padded toward the bathroom, shivering at the loss of body heat. I used the restroom, brushed my teeth, and splashed a bit of water on my face before opening the door, pausing in the hallway. It was so tempting to go back to the couch and snuggle back into Chase's embrace, but I couldn't. I wouldn't. Nothing good would come of that. Falling asleep innocently was one thing, putting myself back out there on purpose was something else entirely. Just as I turned to go into my room, a movement in the dark caught my eye.

Chase was walking towards me, his steady eyes on mine as he moved closer, the sliver of light from the bathroom illuminating our shadows. At his soft, panther-like approach, my instinct had me taking a step backward, bumping into the wall.

He stopped a breath away from me, the heat from his body warming mine, though we weren't yet touching. When I shyly lifted my face toward his, soft brown eyes met mine. He lifted a hand and brushed a piece of hair behind my ear, his fingers leaving a trail of heat across my skin. My breath hitched. And then he reached for me. One of his hands found my cheek, while the other wrapped around my waist, pulling me to him. My arms found their way home on his shoulders, while my hands found his hair. Then his lips were on mine—softly at first. He pulled back to look at me.

Finding no discouragement from me, he kissed me again. This time, the shy meeting of our lips had passed, deepening to something heated. His mouth moved against mine—darting, clinging, tasting. He pressed me closer, trailing tiny kisses across my jaw before returning to taste my lips again. As for me, I clung to him—my fingers in his hair—and desperately wished for the kisses to never end.

Twice he pulled back as if to stop, but a glance at me and our resistance would crumble all over again. He gently pushed me back against the wall with his body. His lips took advantage of my gasp, while his hands held my neck and caressed my face, moving my head to whatever angle would satisfy. Finally, he stepped back, holding me against the wall with one hand as he moved his body away from me.

"You need to stay over there if you don't want me to pull you in over here." He motioned to his doorway and I bit back a smile, even as I flushed, grateful for the dark hallway.

Nearly out of breath, I walked backward toward my room, smiling at him the whole time. "Goodnight, Chase."

His eyes were soft and his voice, a bit huskier than before, said, "Goodnight, Penny."

I stopped. Oh, he had said my name before, but never like *that*. Chills raced down my spine and my stomach tied into knots. The good kind of knots.

The *very* good kind.

"Hold on," I whispered, as I walked back to him, fast and sure. I wrapped my arms around his neck and pulled him down to reach his willing lips. Passion ignited like a flaming arrow between us. His arms banded around my waist as he lifted me up off the ground. Our lips clung and parted together in wild fury for minutes, hours, seconds... I had no idea of the time. When our fire finally slowed to something sweet and tender, I pulled my lips from his, while my feet found solid ground once more.

His eyebrows rose as he kissed me across the lips once more. "Remind me to call you Penny from here on out."

I smiled up at him while he tucked my hair behind my ear. "That's a dangerous game to play."

I pulled out of his embrace and walked backward toward my room, laughing as his grip on my hand tightened and refused to let go of mine. He trailed along after me, but before he could enter my room, I tugged my hand from his grasp.

"Goodnight, Chase!"

He grinned roguishly and stepped back, but as I turned around and entered my room, I felt a light smack on my butt.

I turned around in shock, but he only laughed and said, "If you only knew how long I wanted to do that. 'Night, Blister."

I closed the door, a smile permanently emblazoned across my face.

While sleep was still a *very* long time coming, my dreams were filled with sweetness.

10

Oh, the clarity a morning brings.

When the dawn of a new day chips away at the cozy darkness that came before, perhaps the coziest I'd ever been... Those kisses... My hand rose up to touch my fiery cheeks, just thinking about those kisses with Chase.

I laid in my bed, my door securely locked, though I wasn't sure if I locked it to keep Chase out, or me in. As far as I could hear, the living room was quiet, meaning Chase still slept. I sighed and fluffed my pillow before laying my head back on it again, drawing the covers more tightly around me for warmth.

The name Chase Riley didn't hold much disdain anymore. Now, when I said or thought his name, my heart spiked in rhythm and all I could picture were his hands cupping my face and the look in his eyes before he kissed me.

Stop.

Those eyes though. The hands.

STOP IT.

I drew in a deep breath and tried to clear my head with some quick Zen breathing tricks. The problem was, I didn't know what kissing Chase meant. In high school, he fell into more of the player category. Granted, it was high school, and he was on the football team. He had been popular and good-looking, so it wasn't hard to imagine he'd never be shy of dates. But it had been ten years since then. He may have changed, or he may be the same Chase Riley he had always been.

I was alone with him in a remote cabin. The only interesting, hot-blooded thing around, besides the bears and coyotes, and possibly Bigfoot. I'd be a fool not to consider that I may just be a plaything for him during his vacation. I thought I couldn't stand him before I came to the cabin, and then six days later, I found myself all over him like a bear to honey.

Is that all he was to *me*? A plaything?

I thought about the way my body responded to him as we kissed —heck, every time we touched. Attraction wasn't my issue with Chase. In high school, I hated him so badly, but I would eagerly await Friday nights for the football gang to come to the house for poker. Was it the group of friends that had me applying that extra coat of mascara? Or him?

What about Chase's confession that he liked me in high school? Was that a line? A confession to put me in a better position to gain my trust for a kiss? Why did thrills erupt through my body at his confession? Had I always liked Chase, deep down? Or was I trying to compensate, to make him like me after the dog comment. Had I secretly tried to make him change his mind about me in high school? We were always arguing and debating, ribbing and bashing, but hadn't I been the one to start most of the fights. Was it his attention I had been after?

She looks like my dog, but not as hot.

The words broke through my thoughts and I struggled to remember the feelings they usually invoked inside me, and for the first time, I came up short. The words seemed almost dead to me now. I wasn't a dog. I didn't feel like a dog, especially the way Chase looked at me last night. Maybe those words could finally be put to rest. They'd been proven wrong.

Or had they?

What would happen tomorrow, when he packed up to go home? When our lives separated beyond the cabin? Was all of this just some sort of emotional stress relief between two people locked away together?

I checked my phone for the time and nearly gasped. Ten in the morning. I pulled back the covers and rolled myself out of bed. I had never slept in this long and didn't want to seem like I was hiding out. Especially since that was exactly what I was doing. Was he?

I put my hand on the doorknob, determined to put my roaring feelings aside. When Chase told me our kisses were all in fun or a mistake—I would agree and shake it off. I would be Taylor bloody Swift. We still had a whole day together, and I really wanted to make it as awkward-free as possible. I took several ragged breaths, trying to calm my hyperventilating heart. Why didn't I know what I wanted? Or how I felt? How could I go from a semi-successful woman to a scared, confused, teenager in less than one week? Frustrated with my thoughts, I opened the door and stepped into the hallway.

The house was quiet. Chase's door was closed. I breathed a sigh of relief until I realized he was probably hiding in there too, not wanting to face what we did. Not wanting to face me. I crept into the bathroom. I used the facilities and brushed my teeth. The forgotten mascara of the night before showed in the dark bags beneath my eyes. My lips looked puffy and swollen, the only physical trace of the previous night's sweetness. Well, that and my hair, mussed into something akin to a rat's nest, piled high on my head.

My head was no clearer by the time I had washed my face, applied a fresh coat of mascara, and tamed my hair. I opened the door and walked out into the hallway, immediately noticing Chase's door ajar. He was awake. With deep breaths, a pounding heart, and wearing Chase's oversize sweatpants and a sweatshirt, I trudged closer to the kitchen. I stopped when I saw him. He was leaning against the small kitchen counter, dressed in his basketball shorts and his flannel button-down shirt. His hair was rumpled, and he had his arms folded, peering at nothing, as if deep in thought. He must have sensed my presence and his eyes shifted to mine.

All of a sudden, I knew.

I knew exactly what I wanted. And who I wanted. And very likely, who I had *always* wanted.

He pushed away from the counter and walked toward me. I forced myself to stand still, though my heart spiked. When he reached me, he clutched my face in both hands and kissed me. His lips were soft and warm against mine. The hands that cupped my face were gentle. My heart sang as my surprise wore off, and I quickly wrapped my arms around his neck and pressed close to him. A few long moments later, we came up for air.

"Hi," I said, smiling shyly at him.

He pressed his forehead to mine. "Hey, Blister."

When I opened my mouth to take him to task over his pet name, he kissed me before any words formed, wrapping his arms around me and pressing me close. A moment later, I couldn't for the life of me remember what I was going to tell him. By the time he pulled away, Blister seemed the most romantic endearment to ever grace the earth.

He smiled at me, his eyebrows raised suspiciously. "You weren't hiding back there, were you?"

I scoffed, "Who, me? Of course not. I'm not scared of...anything out here."

Grabbing my hand, he tugged me toward the couch where he sat down, pulling me onto his lap, my legs dangling over his thighs. I sighed as his arms came around me, cradling me against his chest.

"Listen, Pen, I've got to say something," he began, his voice rumbling in my ear. And if you think my heart didn't skyrocket at his shortening of my name, you'd be wrong. "About the dog comment... I honestly don't remember saying it, and I don't know if that makes it better or worse—probably worse. I made you into some sort of four-teen-year-old punchline to impress an idiot, and I wouldn't put it past me back then to do something like that, but I just want you to know, I always liked you. Even back then. I don't think I ever had romantic thoughts about anything but football in the eighth grade, but I remember you in Mr. Thomas's class. I thought you were cool. And obviously, when I got to know you better in high school, I thought you were more than cool. But I'm really sorry that I put you through all that."

His hand stroked my arm as I thought about his words for a moment. I had already made peace with everything, but I appreciated his thoughts. His effort to make something right. The genuine distraught in his tone as he did so. "Thanks, Chase. And I'm really okay." I smiled up at him, placing my hand on his chest. "I'm *very* okay actually, but I appreciate you saying that."

He nodded, his eyes flashing with something sexy, and drew me closer, before I pulled away again to add, "To be fair, I think I got you back in high school."

He laughed. "Actually, that was probably my favorite part."

"Really? I was so horrible to you."

Brushing a hair back from my face, he added, "I don't think you were as mean as you remember. All the insults just made you that much more enticing. Combine that with your hostile, overprotective twin brother and I thought about you all week long. Friday night was my favorite night of the week."

I smiled into his chest, my face ablaze. "Mine too."

And then we were kissing again. All warm and cozy. Seriously though, were his fingers laced with fire? Everywhere he touched left a trail of heat in its wake. So much fire. Too much fire. Chase didn't seem to have the same inhibitions as me. This relationship was new. So new. I guess I could call it a relationship, though we hadn't really given it a name. Actually, we hadn't *talked* much at all, since last night. The last thing I wanted to do was too much too soon and ruin everything. Which meant I had to be extra vigilant with us alone together in the cabin. My breath hitched as he pulled his lips from mine, leaving tiny kisses along my jaw before finding my lips again.

Okay, maybe just another minute or two.

After a few more moments full of complete bliss, I forced myself to pull away from those dang lips. "Do you want to go cut down a Christmas Tree?"

He blinked back at me, as though confused as to why I had pulled away, his eyes still hazy with...desire? I felt my face redden at the thought. A moment later he breathed out a laugh of disbelief, biting his lower lip with his teeth. "How did you know? That is *exactly* what I wanted to do this very second."

I hid my face in his chest again, trying to hide my embarrassed smile, when he cupped my face, tipping my chin up to look at him. He kissed me again, briefly, before he said with a knowing smile, "That's probably a good idea."

After spotting an ax and an old tree stand in the dusty garage, we geared up and spent the rest of the afternoon hunting down the perfect Christmas tree. We held hands, threw snowballs, and made snow angels. At one point, I jumped on his back and he carried me while I nipped at his ear with my teeth. We acted like teenagers, giving all the signs of complete infatuation. Except, when Chase looked at me, there seemed to be more than just admiration in his gaze. Something much deeper, and sweeter shone through. Something that made my heart race and my body tremble. Something that had me thinking about tomorrow.

Our expiration date was stamped on our foreheads. Tomorrow he would leave. He would go back to Eugene to be with his family and then, after that, his life was in Boise. And my life, well I guess technically as a writer it could be anywhere, but it had only been a week. That's crazy, right?

I made it three hours until I couldn't stand the suspense any longer. The not knowing. And really, surviving all the kisses and *accidental* pinches and nudges while we fixed dinner, put the lights on the tree, popped popcorn, and decided on a movie, all the while feeling like I was going to blow a gasket, felt like quite the accomplishment. We were cuddled under a blanket, sitting on the couch, the movie credits beginning to roll, when I could stand it no longer.

"What happens with us after tomorrow?"

Chase coughed, jolting forward on the couch. He had just tossed a handful of popcorn in his mouth. I had impeccable timing. I grinned sheepishly at him while I banged on his back and handed him a glass of water from the coffee table.

After approximately seventeen hours, he could speak again. He paused the movie, leaned back on the couch, his head resting on the headrest, and shifted his eyes toward me.

"That depends. Are we done messing around?"

I held myself still, my lungs waiting for me to give the signal to breathe.

"What do you mean?" My defenses prickled. Was this all messing around to him?

"I know what I want. Do you?"

I opened my mouth but nothing came out. I could only stare at him. Too scared to show my cards until he did first.

He sat up on the couch, his elbows resting on his knees, as he turned toward me. "You're it for me. Even after all this time, I still want what I wanted in high school. I'm not messing around here. I want us to be together. And I'm pretty damn sure I love you."

Ever so slowly, a smile crept across my face, growing bigger and bigger as his words hit home. Was it really going to be this easy? No more games? He seemed to be waiting for some sort of answer, but with his expectant brown eyes peering intently into mine, a bit of shyness overcame me, and I tried hiding my face with my hand.

He grabbed my hand away from my face and pulled us both up and off the couch. His arms wrapped around me, but I quickly tucked my face into his chest.

"Hey, no hiding. What are you thinking?"

Smiling into his shoulder, I lifted my head up and whispered, "Same."

"Same?"

"Yeah."

He scoffed, even as his face lit up and he pulled me closer. "I bare my heart and soul to you and all I get is 'same?' You're the writer."

I poked my finger into the side of his stomach, laughing as he squirmed. "You're right, should I think of four more sentences?"

"Brat."

Only when our kisses slowed, my head resting on his chest while my body molded against him, did I whisper, "I'm pretty sure I love you too."

He smiled and squeezed me tighter. His mouth came down on mine. With one hand, he cupped my face while the other pressed me closer. This time, the flavor of his kiss was sweeter than ever before. This time, his kiss tasted of promise; of devotion. It tasted like teasing eyes and a crooked smile. It tasted like nine to five and a house full of babies. It tasted like forever.

Then I felt something scurry across my foot.

Scurry.

There was only one thing that *scurried* anywhere. I broke away from Chase in time to see a small rodent scampering into the hallway. And it had *touched* me.

Immediately, I started jumping up and down, squealing. Chase looked both confused and alarmed at my sudden outburst. I pointed toward the hallway. "Mouse. Ran over my *foot!*"

For a brief moment, we were both hopping up and down, clutching each others' hands, literally freaking out, for lack of a better term. Chase must have realized what that looked like and finally pulled us both onto the couch.

"Matt and Gina are going to get some serious points knocked off their rental profile," he said, as his eyes scanned the room.

My hand flew to my cheek. "I left my bedroom door open." Stick a fork in me, I was done. Officially never getting off this couch.

His horrified gaze met mine. "Me too."

He looked so alarmed I had to laugh, even though my plight felt just as desperate. "What *happened* to you?"

"You don't want to know."

"I guess this means you're not going to save the day?"

He glowered at me as he tickled the side of my stomach. I laughed and tried to turn away, only to have him pull me in closer.

"I vote we pretend the floor is lava and we don't get off this couch all night," Chase said, his eyes trained on the hallway.

"That seems dangerous. Although very probable since I won't be getting off this couch until Helga is dead."

"Helga?"

"Harold's girlfriend. Out for revenge. Seemed appropriate."

"It fits. Alright. New plan. We stay up all night watching movies and we don't leave this couch." He eyed me suspiciously. "No funny business. Just movies."

I smacked his chest. Apparently, he had more faith in my bladder than I did, as well as my self-control. But I thought I could probably handle both for the night. A mouse running wild about the house, probably rummaging through all my things at the moment, did not scream romance to me.

I smiled. "Sounds perfect. You grab the remote."

At his confused look, I pointed to where the remote lay next to the TV, after being flung across the room in our mouse frenzy.

He groaned.

I awoke feeling cozy and in love, but with a crick in my neck. Chase and I had fallen asleep on the couch. We had been nicely barricaded off the ground so Harold's family couldn't have access to us. I'd be lying if I said I didn't have to pee, but bad experience or not, I would be making Chase go first. I had to have some girlfriend perks. The TV in front of us showed a blue screen, which had, long ago, gone silent after our third movie of the night. The lighted Christmas tree in the corner gave off the most beautiful, cozy atmosphere, and I realized that today was Christmas. I looked at Chase from where I lay next to him and began kissing his lips, soft and slow. He smiled, tightening his arms around me, without opening his eyes.

"Merry Christmas, Blister."

I smiled, reaching out to pinch him when all of a sudden the front door swung wide open, slamming into the wall. Chase and I both startled, turning our heads to see who or what was about to enter.

Matt entered the cabin, keys dangling in his hand while he set down a load of luggage. He eyed us on the couch, almost triumphantly. "Hey, guys."

Two small bodies, one boy and one girl raced inside the room, holding toys and shouting "Aunt Penny! Aunt Penny! It's Christmas!"

I laughed and gave awkward hugs to my niece and nephew as they piled on top of me and Chase, showing us all the race cars and babies and toys their chubby hands were holding.

"What time is it?" I asked Matt, confused as to how they could have already opened their presents at home and still gotten here so fast.

"It's eleven." Matt raised his eyebrows and folded his arms, looking very amused. "And when your demon children wake up at 4:30 am to open presents, it makes our timing much more doable." He gave us each a pointed look. "Looks like you both had a good night."

I pulled myself up to a sitting position, trying to tame my wild hair, while Chase folded his arms behind his head and grinned.

Gina stepped through the doorway last, pulling a large suitcase behind her, a duffle bag strapped across her chest. "Well, it's safe to say Penny's car is stuck until spring. We had to park below and hike up..." Her voice trailed off as she spotted us together on the couch. A slow smile of satisfaction appeared on her face.

Matt smiled and sauntered over to his wife, helping to relieve her of her duffle bag and coat. "I'm sure we all have lots to catch up on, but first..." He pointed toward me and Chase on the couch and gave his wife a kiss on the cheek. "Gina, you owe me fifty bucks."

CONFESSIONS
FROM THE AUTHOR, PENNY RILEY

1. Matt knew he had double booked the cabin. He always felt bad about not encouraging his friend to pursue his sister, even though it would have been weird. He also knew they were both single. So, when Chase wanted to use the cabin and he knew Penny had nowhere to go for the week, he and Gina made it happen. They only wished they could have been there to watch the sparks fly for those first few days.

2. Chase really did have a crush on Penny in high school. He became friends with Matt in an effort to get to know her and, if not to date her, then to be able to annoy her weekly. You know, the boys and pulling pigtails theory. But he ended up really enjoying Matt's friendship and they became best friends.

3. That was indeed Penny's Jack of hearts. If he had played the hand he had been given, Chase would have won with a straight flush. He discretely dropped one of his cards on the floor and picked up a random card on the table, which just so happened to be Penny's discarded Jack. Chase

cheated so Penny could save face and win some dang clothes. Swoon.

4. Upon closer, internal inspection, Penny also had a crush on Chase in high school.

5. Chase had been eight years old. He had been invited to a birthday sleepover party at a friend's house. The group of boys had slept down in the basement. Somewhere between the time Chase fell asleep that night and woke up the next morning, there were four mice sleeping next to his feet at the bottom of his warm sleeping bag. Early that morning, still half asleep, he felt an itch on his ankle. He scratched it. Another itch. He scratched it again. He was more awake at this point. He then felt the swish of something long and wiry, and very much like a tail, brush against his entire leg. His eyes snapped open in alarm and in one swift movement, he scrambled out of his bag, screaming in horror. The next twenty seconds were full of mad chaos as both boys and mice clambered about the room in confusion and terror. A bad experience, indeed.

6. It wasn't a blister. It was a pimple. Very large and gushy and at the end of her fourteen-year-old nose. She didn't know she could pop it. Her mom had once told her if she popped a zit, it would leave a large hole in her face, and then it would grow back even larger. So, she left it. She was young and innocent. She was at a freshman dance with Gina when she got bumped in the nose and it exploded. EXPLODED. It had not been pretty. Blister really was a generous nickname.

7. Penny did get her book finished and into her editor on time. She also finished an autobiographical novella about her time at the cabin with Chase. She called it, 'A Christmas Spark.'

The End

ALSO BY CINDY STEEL

Pride and Pranks Series

A Christmas Spark (Chase & Penny)

That Fine Line (Cade & Kelsey)

Stranded Ranch (Dusty & Lucy)

Double or Nothing (Logan & Tessa)

ACKNOWLEDGMENTS

First and foremost: my husband and kiddos. I hope I can continue to prove to all of us that I can be a real author one day. And James, thanks for letting me sleep in occasionally, after a late night of writing.

My mom and sister. Thank you for inspiring me to write a fun, cliche, Hallmark holiday romance as a Christmas present to you both. I had so much fun, I think I'll do a few more! This story has come a long way since then, but thanks for loving it as much as I did.

My critique group! One of the best things I have ever done was to put my timid self out there enough to be part of a critique group. You guys have taught me so much, given me great ideas for my stories, and been excited with me. It means the world! Karen—thanks so much for your helpful ideas, late-night chats, and critiques.

My Beta and ARC readers! Thank you for taking a chance on a new author, reading my book, and telling your friends. It means so much to me.

My editor, Hayleigh Burnett at The Editing Fox. Thanks for being so kind in your edits and for your ideas to make this story really shine.

Amy Romney - Thank you for proofreading!

My Cover Designer, Lorri at Pure Art Digital. Thanks for taking an idea and bringing it to life so beautifully.

And finally...you! If you are reading this, thank you so much! This sweet and silly romance was so fun to write. It's not Shakespeare, it probably won't change your life, but I really, really hope it made you smile.

ABOUT CINDY

Cindy Steel was raised on a dairy farm in Idaho. She grew up singing country songs at the top of her lungs and learning to solve all of life's problems while milking cows and driving tractors—rewriting happy endings every time. She married a cute Idaho boy and is the proud mother of two wild and sweet twin boys. Which means she is also now a collector of bugs, sticks, rocks, and slobbery kisses. She loves making breakfast, baking, photography, reading a good book, and staying up way past her bedtime to craft stories that will hopefully make you smile.

She loves to connect and get to know her readers! She is the most active on Instagram at @authorcindysteel, Facebook at Author Cindy Steel, and her website is www.cindysteel.com.

Made in United States
Troutdale, OR
11/28/2023

15052562R00066